D0282911

The Taxi Navigator

The Taxi Navigator

RICHARD MOSHER

DEC 12 1996

PHILOMEL BOOKS ✦ NEW YORK

CONN LIBRARY
Wayne State College
1111 Main Street
Wayne, NE 68787

Patricia Lee Gauch, Editor

Text copyright © 1996 by Richard Mosher. All rights reserved.
Maps on cover © 1996 by Rand McNally, R.L. 96-S-33
This book, or parts thereof, may not be reproduced in any form without permission in writing from the publisher, Philomel Books, a division of The Putnam & Grosset Group, 200 Madison Avenue, New York, NY 10016.
Philomel Books, Reg. U. S. Pat. & Tm. Off.
Published simultaneously in Canada.
Printed in the United States. Type design by Gunta Alexander.
The text is set in New Baskerville.
Library of Congress Cataloging-in-Publication Data
Mosher, Richard. The taxi navigator : a novella / by Richard Mosher.
p. cm. Summary: As his lawyer father and banker mother become increasingly estranged a boy finds solace with his taxicab driver uncle and a group of somewhat eccentric friends. [1. Uncles—Fiction.
2. Taxicabs—Fiction. 3. Family problems—Fiction. 4. Friendship—Fiction.
5. Death—Fiction. 6. Grief—Fiction. 7. New York (N.Y.)—Fiction.] I. Title.
PZ7.M8485Tax 1996 [Fic]—dc20 96-11687 CIP AC
ISBN 0-399-23104-8
1 3 5 7 9 10 8 6 4 2
First Impression

For Chris,
who was the first to know

Contents

1
Hoboken Time

Even when I was a little kid, it was easy to see the difference between my parents and my Uncle Hank. For example, they said very different things about being scared of the dark. My dad said it was okay for me to be scared sometimes, but not when I was in bed and supposed to be asleep. He didn't understand how my bed, even with all its blankets and toys, could still be a scary place. My mom said I was smart to be scared of the dark now and then, like when we were outside at night and someone might mug us. But Uncle Hank said it was also smart to be friends with the dark, because the dark could be sweet and could whisper secrets to us if we listened.

Uncle Hank was an expert on the dark. He was a

cabdriver and he worked the night shift, driving up and down Manhattan—and Brooklyn and Queens too—until only a few grown-ups were still out. If they were too scared to ride a subway train, they stood by the curb, with one hand in the air, and waited for him to drive them home. So Uncle Hank wasn't scared of the dark. Except sometimes, he said, when he wouldn't mind having a smart taxi-kid like me riding along to help him see farther out into the night.

We went for rides together in his taxi, on Sunday afternoons long ago when I was still in first grade and he was so young his hair didn't have any white in it.

But then Uncle Hank took his taxi money and went away to places I'd never heard of, and I didn't see him for years. Every month a postcard arrived, addressed to me, Kid Kyle, showing a blond boy skiing down a glacier, or a brown boy leading a donkey cart, or a black boy, with nothing on, diving far down to a pale green sea. Still I couldn't quite believe he was so far away, and whenever I saw a taxi I looked to see if it might be him at the wheel.

One summer passed, then a year of second grade, and another summer, and a year of third grade, and then *another* summer—until I had almost forgotten what Uncle Hank looked like. Then he came back and I saw him again. He wasn't quite so tall as I remembered, and he had tried fooling us by growing a beard that made his face look long and his eyes look sad.

"You've got some dandy white hairs in that bush," said my dad, who hated the gray in his own hair. "Looks distinguished."

"Sure." Uncle Hank smiled, but the sadness didn't leave his eyes.

"But you're so *thin,*" said my mom. "Didn't they feed you over there?"

"Of course they did. But I didn't eat as much as we eat here, or as often—and I walked a lot. Wherever I went, the people said they were surprised to meet an American who walked so much."

"You didn't drive?" I asked softly, shy of his new face.

"No. Except when I was driven, you know, in buses or trains. But mostly I walked."

This was a great disappointment. Through all the years of his absence, I had imagined Uncle driving from place to place in a car very much like a yellow cab, sometimes alone, sometimes with a beautiful dark woman, and sometimes with passengers. I was almost afraid to ask my next question. "Then are you going to walk here, too? You aren't going to drive?"

"I don't know yet." He spoke very slowly. "Maybe I should become a lawyer."

Hearing this, my dad, who was a lawyer himself,

turned a bit pink. "It's not too late. To become a lawyer, I mean, or to become—something."

"Oh, I think it's always been too late for me to do those sorts of things. But what do *you* think, Kid Kyle?" Uncle Hank looked straight at me. "Do you think I should drive again?"

"Yes," I said, and wondered why my parents didn't look as glad as I felt. "I think you should drive a cab like before. And if you love walking so much, you can still do that too, can't you?"

"Yes, New York is a fine place for walking. And what else should I do, along with driving a cab?"

"Cut off your beard."

Now they all laughed, Dad especially.

"Maybe." Uncle Hank nodded. "But only if you can give me a good reason. Why should I cut it off?"

"Because it makes you look sad. You should look happy, Uncle Hank."

His eyebrows arched high when I said this, and his eyes sparkled with the old teasing look I had nearly forgotten. "Well, you're right! I should look happy! And you say shaving off my beard would do it?"

I rocked my head up and down.

"You're *sure?*"

"Well—" I could tell he was teasing a little more now, and my dad was laughing too loud, the way he did sometimes when he'd had lots to drink and Mom was nervous and said he should stop. "You can look sad if you want to, Uncle." I didn't go look for the scissors.

A few weeks later, on a Saturday, I was standing in the bathroom when Mom and Dad thought I was asleep. They were sitting in the kitchen drinking coffee.

"Have you noticed," Dad began, "how Kyle's changed since our hero came back from Morocco?"

"Yes. He's more talkative now—"

"More talkative? He never stops! I know it's good for a kid to express himself—but the *ideas* Hank gives him! They aren't—"

"Safe?" Mom's voice was gentle, as if she weren't talking to an adult but to a kid even younger than I was. "No, maybe they aren't safe. But Kyle's bound to meet teachers with ideas we don't like, and other parents who have ideas we don't like. Religious ideas, political ideas—"

"I don't mean politics. Politics I can deal with. I mean hopes and dreams—the sort of dreams Hank has, that don't come to anything." Dad sounded tired, like when he came home late and was impatient with everything, even with Mom, until he finished his first martini. "I don't want my son growing up to be a cabdriver."

"But, George, he's only nine years old. We should let him be a boy for a few years before he starts concentrating on money."

"It's much more than *money,*" said Dad. "It's how people will see him, and what they'll think of him—"

"Mostly," Mom answered, "it's money." And I thought she should know, because she was a banker and knew everything about money. Staring at my face in the bathroom mirror, I wished I hadn't heard any of their talk. Then Dad spoke again.

"We need to organize Kyle to see that he goes to good places, and learns good values—"

"What we *need,*" said Mom's low voice, "is some time to ourselves. We work so hard at our jobs, and then, when we get home—"

I heard her sigh. All the way from the bathroom I heard her sigh, deeply, twice.

"—When we get home," Dad finished for her, "it's another whole job dealing with *him.* Isn't that the truth."

I covered my ears so I wouldn't hear what they said next. The bathroom door was open; I tiptoed up the stairs to my bed.

Uncle Hank asked a funny question when I told him the things I'd overheard—because I did tell him, the next time I went riding in his cab with him. He watched the traffic ahead of us and watched the flashing Don't Walk sign beneath the traffic light. Then he said, "Kyle, are you sure you weren't dreaming?"

"I was wide awake, Uncle. They said they were tired of me."

"No, what I think they said was that you're a nine-year-old kid with energetic ideas, and they can't keep up with you when they get home from work."

"They don't love me." I was amazed to hear the words leave my mouth.

"Of course they love you—they love you so much they want what's best for you. Remember how your dad keeps saying I should drive you to the museum?"

"Sure I remember." Week after week, Uncle and I had promised my parents we would go visit it—but something more fun always happened instead. "The Museum of Natural History. First they say I should go there. Then they say that they wish I didn't have to go there in your cab."

Uncle smiled, his eyes focused on the traffic light. "Maybe they think my cab is dangerous."

"But not if you drive carefully and wear your seat belt. And you told me yourself that if you steer clear of those other cars—"

"I mean dangerous in other ways. Dangerous because if you grew up to be a cabdriver, like I am, you might want to travel, like I do, to faraway countries—"

"But Uncle, so what?"

"So if you traveled, you wouldn't have money for other things. A house, and fine clothes—"

"And money for—children?"

"That's right, kids cost money too, though not in the same way."

"And how about money for *girlfriends,* Uncle?"

"I don't know what you're talking about." Maybe he didn't but he was smiling anyway. "Seems to me, I haven't had a girlfriend in ages."

"That's not what Mom says."

"Well, when it comes to talking about uncles and girlfriends, sometimes moms exaggerate."

"But don't girlfriends cost money, Uncle? I mean, for perfume and valentines and all that kind of stuff?"

"Maybe they do. It's been such a long time, I hardly recall. *Money,*" grunted Uncle Hank. "Money, money, money." He scowled across the lanes of traffic to Madison Avenue's fancy shops. Then he grinned back at me. "Let's make up a song about money, so we don't have to worry about it. All right, Kid?"

"All right." Making up songs was one of our Sunday specialties.

But before we thought of even one song-word to rhyme with money, we turned left onto Seventy-ninth Street, and I saw the woman standing at the corner of Fifth Avenue, her hand held high.

"She wants a cab, Uncle."

"I know, but this cab is off duty. The light on top even says so. I promised your parents I would take you to the museum for a shot of good straight education."

"But she isn't going far—"

"Oh? And how do you know that?" We inched toward the woman on the corner. There were lots of cabs ahead of us, but none stopped to pick her up.

"I know because she has the Fifth Avenue Look." This was a term I'd heard Uncle Hank use for certain women. "Doesn't she, Uncle? Isn't she going just a few blocks down Fifth Avenue?"

"I'm not so sure. But here, I'll tell you what. If her paw is still in the air when we get to the corner, and if no other cab wants her first, we'll stop and take her."

"Even if I'm wrong about her Fifth Avenue Look?"

"Even if she's going to Timbuktu." He smiled.

There were taxis honking all around us, but they must all have been carrying passengers because they rolled past the woman without stopping. In one hand she held a big red shopping bag—and her other hand, when we reached the corner, was waving directly at us.

"Oh, taxi!" she screeched. "Taxi, taxi, pleeease stop!"

We did, two feet in front of her. She sprawled into the back seat.

I turned to face her and asked, "Where are you going, please?"

"A kid," she said thickly. "A *kid* driving a cab. Now I've seen all there is to see in th—"

"Where are you going?" asked Uncle Hank, the way my music teacher talked when she'd had enough nonsense. "Down Fifth Avenue or where?"

"I'm going," said the lady, her breath smelling like fresh paint, or like my dad when he'd had too much to drink, "I'm *going* to Hoboken."

"Well that's terrific." Uncle Hank gave me a narrow smile, and I smiled back—I had ridden with him enough to know that Hoboken was clear across the Hudson River in New Jersey. "I *thought* you had the Jersey Voice." When he winked at me, I winked back—she might *look* Fifth Avenue, but she sure didn't sound it. Then he said over his shoulder, "I hope you realize Hoboken costs you double the meter, plus three dollars for my return toll?"

"I *reelize,*" snorted the woman, as if she had mud in her mouth. "I *reelize* all about it. Don't act smart. Doubla meter, doubla meter, swell. Twenny-five, twenny-six bucks. *Got* it?"

"Got it." Uncle Hank headed us down Fifth Avenue. "Here we go. So much for the museum and the high-class education."

"How's that?" Her eyes, when I turned to see why she was shouting, were pink and watery like a rabbit's. "Jeez, this driver looks about eight. Seen it all now." She fell back into her corner and sighed a huge sigh and, before I could believe it, was snoring. Not loud like in the cartoons but weak and wet and blubbery.

"She's out, Nephew. Can you beat that?"

"Is she—is she drunk?"

"Yes, I'd say she's drunk as a coot."

"But how could she be, Uncle! It's only—only—" And here I had some trouble, because although I saw a clock right on Fifth Avenue, I couldn't quite read it as we sailed by. Even after my ninth birthday, I had some trouble telling time.

Uncle Hank helped me. "I know what you mean—it's only three o'clock."

"How could she be drunk at three o'clock?"

"She probably had a drink or two for breakfast, then a couple more for lunch. When we drop her in Hoboken, she'll be ready for teatime. But she does have a sweet snore—almost as sweet a noise as our meter." He tapped the square metal machine in front of me. "Our cash creator. Every click of this meter is a quarter for us—and this trip it's *two* quarters, since we're going to Jersey and will collect double."

We curved into the long bright tube of the tunnel. Its lights washed over us—and, along with the swaying motion of our taxi, made me feel almost dizzy. But it didn't wake the woman in back.

"Uncle, is everyone you drive around New York as angry as this lady?"

"Not at all. And it's got nothing to do with the Fifth Avenue Look or the Jersey Voice. Some people are born in a bad mood and stay in it, rich or poor, smart or dumb. You're right, this one's on the difficult side—she might even prove difficult when it comes time to pay. Still, you never know with drunks. She might give us a hundred dollars as her own sort of joke."

"She *might?*"

"Anything's possible, although a seventy-five-dollar tip does seem unlikely."

"What's the idea of a tip, Uncle?"

"Oh, it's meant to be a reward for giving the passenger a good ride. A bonus. They don't really have to pay it, but mostly they do." We flashed out into the sunlight, then into another tunnel, much shorter than the first. "Hey, Lady!" called Uncle Hank, not too roughly, but roughly enough to stop her snoring. "Lady, it's time you told us where you're going."

"Hoboken," she sputtered. "Hoboken, New Jhhhersey."

"But where in Hoboken? Should I go left, go right?"

"Go straight, Bud," she said, even though his name wasn't Bud. "I'll show you the turn."

And she did, and we arrived at her brick apartment house, bigger than my brownstone in Brooklyn but not so big as Uncle Hank's building in Manhattan.

When he pushed the same button he had pushed to start the meter, the clicking stopped. "With our return toll, it comes to twenty-four-fifty."

"Jeez, that's a lot." She scrambled out the door and

lowered her bag to the sidewalk. "Willikers. That's a lot for a cab ride."

"Yep." Uncle Hank nodded. "But you knew it would be a lot. You said as much when we picked you up."

"I did?"

"Just pay, please, and we'll drive back to the city."

"Awrrright." She opened her purse, shook it, and handed me a five-dollar bill. Then she peered closer at my face. "Awful young to be driving a cab."

"I'm sitting on the wrong side to be the driver," I said, but she didn't seem to hear me.

"Yes, Kyle's a taxi whiz," said Uncle Hank. "A genius. But this isn't twenty-four dollars, or even twenty."

"No?" She patted one coat pocket and another until she had patted them all. "Too bad, because it's all I've got, that one fin and I'm busted. But inside the house I've got a bottle of whiskey. I'll bring you a bottle of whiskey." She picked up her shopping bag.

"No whiskey," said Uncle Hank. "Inside the house, have you got cash?"

"Sure, plenty of cash inside. You don't want whiskey?"

"Go get the cash," he said, as if talking to a kindergartner. "Nineteen-fifty, you owe us. But leave something here when you go. Leave your overcoat."

"I *love* my overcoat." Her lower lip trembled.

"Then leave your purse."

"That's it—I'll leave you my wallet."

"Good," said Uncle Hank. "Your wallet. Very good."

"No, wait. Not my wallet. My *watch*. I'll leave you my watch."

"Fine. Leave your watch with my navigator, then bring the nineteen-fifty you still owe us."

It took her a while to unfasten the watch from her wrist, but finally she handed it through the side window. Then she grabbed her shopping bag and disappeared into the building.

We waited.

"Will she come back, Uncle?" The watch was gold and pretty and felt warm in my hand.

"She might. Hard to say. But tell me—is this trip as interesting as a museum?"

"It's more fun than any museum."

"Fun, sure. But is it interesting? Is it—educational? I mean, what would my brother George think of us sitting in Hoboken, waiting for some drunken babe to cough up twenty bucks?"

"He might not like it, I guess."

"No, I guess he might not. So maybe we'd better not tell him, okay?"

"Okay, Uncle. Or Mom either, right?"

Uncle Hank winced. "I guess not."

"I don't like lying to Mom. Or Dad."

"Well I'm glad you feel that way."

"But Uncle, is it a lie when I don't tell them something? I mean, instead of saying a thing that isn't true?"

"In a way," said Uncle Hank. "And in a way not. Even your father the lawyer would have a ticklish time with that one. There are different sides of the truth."

Before I could ask what "different sides of the truth" meant, the woman staggered out of her building. Holding a bottle in one hand, she made her way to Uncle Hank's window.

"Here, Bud. A bottle of white wine."

"So I see. But it's worth maybe three dollars, and I asked for nineteen-fifty. Anyway, I don't drink." He squeezed my shoulder to keep me quiet.

"Don't *drink?*" She stared at him. "You're so lucky."

"Yes, I suppose I am. But now I need cash, please, and the sooner the better—this isn't a charity operation. And remember, we've got your watch."

"Oh, right. My slinky Timex. I owe you nineteen bucks?"

"Plus the tip," I piped up, "since we gave you a good ride."

"Jeez, now he wants a tip." She turned back to her building.

"That was good, Kyle, very good. We should be partners in this racket."

"Okay. I'll quit school, and we can drive around New York all day."

"All *night,* you mean—my shift usually *begins* about now. But I don't think your folks would enjoy having you cruise New York, even for tips. Why don't you try on the watch? It's small enough that it just might fit you."

"It isn't mine, Uncle. It belongs to the drunk lady."

"Not if she doesn't bring our twenty dollars. Go ahead, try it on. It'll fit you if we punch another hole in the strap."

We waited ten minutes, but the woman didn't arrive. Then we waited another ten minutes while Uncle Hank explained the sort of things we might have seen at the Museum of Natural History, in case Mom or Dad had questions. The more he talked—about the dinosaur skeletons and the cougars and leopards—the more interesting the place sounded.

"Good," he said. "We'll give it a visit sometime. But now that you have such a pretty watch, maybe I should help you learn to read it better. According to your taxi watch, the time in Hoboken is, let's see, exactly ten after four."

"But isn't she coming back, Uncle?"

"She is not coming back. Remember how fast she fell asleep, crossing Manhattan? She's snoring that same tune this instant, up in her apartment. Hoboken Time is exactly eleven after four, and we're on our way back to the city."

As we pulled out from the curb I admired the gold watch sliding up and down my arm. "But, Uncle, how many sides of the truth are there?"

"As many as there are people. Don't worry too much about it, is my advice. Just do what feels right."

And then, through the long white tunnel, Uncle Hank explained what my teachers had explained so many times in the past, about the big hand and the little hand, and how they told time. And finally, in the magic of our bouncing, squeaking yellow taxicab, it all began to make sense.

2

Warlock on Wheels

My dad was always very busy, working for a big law firm in Manhattan. He said the place was called Snorkel, Bork, Trample, and Toad, but I knew he was teasing. And even if he made fun of his firm's name, what he wanted most was to be made a partner there. But to do that, he had to work harder and better than all the other men and women who also wanted to be made partners. So he worked endless days and weeks and months.

This meant that all through the summer he could never quite take me roller-skating in Central Park, since at the last minute he always had to fly off to California or someplace for his law firm. It was okay, he explained, because his traveling was necessary for him to become a partner. Someday, he said, someday soon, he would have lots of time for me.

He was a good dad, I guess, just very busy. Finally, a week after the lady in Hoboken left me her gold-colored watch, he felt so bad about not taking me roller-skating that he let Uncle Hank take me—even though he didn't think Uncle Hank was safe. Safe for me, I mean, since Uncle Hank was a cabdriver and Dad didn't want me growing up to be a cabdriver; he wanted me to be a lawyer like *he* was. Mom said I shouldn't be expected to think like a grown-up yet because I was still only nine. But Dad agreed Uncle Hank could take me, even after all the trouble the Hoboken watch had caused. (Or the trouble it *would* have caused, if Uncle hadn't called and explained to Dad that my watch made up for the money the drunk lady hadn't paid us.)

His taxi was at our curb at 2:06, and off we flew. The cables of the Brooklyn Bridge spun past like parts of a huge spider web shining in the sun.

"Pilot to Navigator," called Uncle Hank. "What's our time, Kid?"

I checked my dial. "Hoboken Time is exactly, ah, seventeen minutes after two o'clock. And what's our speed, Pilot?"

"Velocity fifty hundred miles an hour—if we go any

velociter we'll spin out of orbit. Please advise as to our route, Navigator. Maybe onto the highway, then up to Sixty-first Street, and then west to Wollman Rink, our roller-skating headquarters?"

"Sounds good to me, Pilot."

"Roger," he said with a snap. "Over."

"Over and out."

We zoomed under the Manhattan Bridge and then the Williamsburg Bridge; on the East River a ski-plane took off and grew smaller and smaller as it flew far behind us in the direction of Brooklyn.

We made it to Central Park without stopping for even one drunken woman. At Wollman Rink, which sits in the middle of the park, we rented skates—and kneepads for when we fell down. And I would fall down plenty, since it was the first time I ever went roller-skating.

Away we rolled, then, on one of the long curving paths. Central Park was so big I could hardly believe it could fit into a place as crowded as New York, but there it was, all green and fresh smelling, with hills and baseball diamonds and miles and miles of curving paths.

Our first hill was no work until it stopped going down and went up, and I slipped and tripped and Uncle Hank had to give me a pull. We huffed to the top and coasted to the bottom, then fell back on a bench for some rest.

"So," Uncle Hank asked, "How's school these days? Any fun?"

"Sometimes." On a tree across the path from us, a few high branches had already turned orange. "Sure, it's fun sometimes. But—I'm scared."

Maybe Uncle Hank understood that a kid can be scared of something without knowing *why* it scares him. He didn't ask, the way my dad would have. He gazed peacefully up at the orange branches.

"I'm scared," I said, when I was ready, "of talking to the kids I want to talk to the most."

"Lonely." Uncle Hank nodded, as if being lonely was the most natural condition in life, or as if it didn't surprise him that I could be lonely even though I had lived in Brooklyn for years. "Lonely, lonely, lonely. Have you told your mother about being lonely for these best friends you don't have?"

"Uncle, how could I? She worries too much already, about me, about Dad, about her problems at work—"

"Too bad you don't have a turtle."

"Give me a break. A *turtle?*"

"When I was a kid," he smiled, "I had a stuffed turtle named Sam."

"But you also had a brother. My dad."

"That's true enough. Still, there were plenty of

things I couldn't tell anyone but Sam the turtle. And if I had Sam now, even he wouldn't be enough. Many people are lonely, Kyle. I'm lonely myself."

"But, Uncle, you can't be lonely! You have all your girlfriends!"

"All *what* girlfriends?"

"The ones Mom talks about. She says you have a different girlfriend every week, and you live a crazy life because it's so jumbled up—"

"Sometimes, even your mother can bend the truth." Uncle Hank smiled. He reached for his empty shirt pocket, like Dad reaching for a cigarette. "I don't think she's met a single girlfriend of mine."

"She met the one at the train station, with the blue scarf, who bought me cotton candy—"

"What a memory, Kid. That was years ago."

"You haven't had a girlfriend since her?"

"I don't quite remember." He leaned over to tighten one of my laces. "Not every week, I haven't. Not last week or the week before or the week before that—"

"Maybe this week," I said, hoping to take away some of his loneliness and mine, too. "Maybe you'll meet her in the park this afternoon."

"Maybe," said Uncle Hank. "But I doubt it."

"Are there lots of girls in the park?" As if I didn't know.

"Millions. We'll find just the one for you."

"Not for *me,* Uncle. I don't like girls."

He only laughed and watched the branches.

Two black boys skated by, one dancing under a giant radio while the other twisted and whirled, making it look too easy. A redheaded girl, kneepads grimy and eyes wide, tottered past us, then up and up until she, too, vanished over the hill. For a moment there was no one. Then a woman in purple sailed over the rise, and at first I thought she was a young woman—young, I mean, the way Uncle Hank was young—because her hair streamed out behind her, and she skated so gracefully down to us.

Then I saw that her hair was all white, and her eyes as pale blue as the sky—and zip, she was past us, skimming away in long strides, white hair floating back toward me. But she didn't skate over the hill; she didn't disappear. Instead, she made a swooping easy turn and glided back in our direction as gently as a purple-feathered bird.

"Isn't she afraid of skinning herself, Uncle? She doesn't have kneepads."

"Maybe she doesn't need them, since she skates so well. Or maybe—"

He went silent as the old woman drew near. To my fearful delight, she stopped skating right in front of me, then peered at me with her friendly blue eyes.

"Why are you staring?" she asked softly. "Am I that ugly?"

If I hadn't been embarrassed, I might have said I was

staring because she was beautiful, except that when she spoke I saw she lacked some front teeth and wasn't beautiful at all.

"Don't answer, then." She smiled. "Be rude on top of impolite. But at least you'll let me share your bench?"

I couldn't say a word.

"I must admit, you *are* a cute snip, even with your manners missing. So I'll sit here with you and your equally cute papa and give my ticker a rest." She sat on the bench beside me.

"He isn't my papa." I studied the treetops in the hope of looking calm. "He's my uncle and I'm his nephew. Why don't you wear kneepads?"

"Because I don't fall, is why. I've got balance. Do you have balance?"

"Not much, I guess. But this is only my first day."

"Then you'll *get* balance, you'll be a skating wizard, a warlock, a—"

"A warlock?"

"Yes. A boy witch. I'm kind of a witch myself, so of course I skate well. Yes, I can see you'll be a skating warlock in no time."

"Witches," I informed her, "ride brooms."

"So old-fashioned! Certainly I have a broom, but I leave it in the pantry. A modern witch needs wheels."

"You can't be a witch. You're too nice."

"But my dear boy, there are nice witches and nasty

ones. We aren't all bad!" She burst into a low laugh, and I saw that not all her front teeth were out, only one. And she *was* beautiful, even with the gap in her mouth and her white hair and the wrinkles around her eyes. "Shall I show you how to skate with balance?"

"Yes, please. But Uncle Hank has to come with us."

"I know, I know—mustn't speak with strangers, especially in Central Park. A most sensible rule—I can see that your parents are filled with good caution. This uncle I'm not so sure of, but he may skate along with us. He might profit from some balance himself."

Now that I had heard her laugh, speaking to her was easy. "No, Witch—what Uncle really needs is a girlfriend. We've been looking all afternoon."

"That only requires another sort of balance." The woman in purple got up and pulled me up with her. "But don't call me Witch out here in public—it lets the others know. My name is Marcella. And I've been more or less introduced to your silent uncle, but I don't know *your* name, Little Wisdom. It is—?"

"Kid Kyle. Kid Kyle the—the Warlock Navigator."

"Excellent." She took my right hand and Uncle Hank took my left. "Since you navigate, you shall decide whether we go uphill or down. And since I balance, you shall hold my hand."

After I chose to skate up the hill, she gave a tug and off we rolled, steadily uphill with hardly any effort. It was all in the lightness of your stride, said Marcella, and in the strength of your spirit. I wasn't sure what she meant by this, but skating beside her was so much easier than skating any other way—and so much more fun—that she must have been telling the truth.

When it was time for her "ticker" to take another rest, we sat on a bench and caught our breath and listened to the whispering trees.

Marcella turned to Uncle Hank. "Stranger, it's time we talked. Your name is Hank?"

"So they say."

"What do you do, Hank?"

"I drive a cab."

"Intriguing." She gave him such a strong look that I almost reminded her staring wasn't polite. "But," she insisted, "what do you *do?*"

"Nothing much," said Uncle Hank. "Sometimes I go out taxi-exploring with Kid Kyle here—"

"And he travels," I put in, "whenever he has the money. And he writes long weird stories he won't show my mom and dad."

"Ah," Marcella sighed. "And he has no girlfriend?"

"Not this week. Me neither. The difference is, Uncle Hank likes girls and I don't."

"I see." Marcella shook herself as if awakening from a nap. "Well, it's time I made my way home."

"Do you skate home?"

"Child, not in these times. From here it's either the IRT local—you know, the subway train—or the bus."

"But why don't you skate? Did you rent skates like we did, so you have to give them back?"

"That's not why." For a moment her eyes shone as purple as her cloak. "No, these skates are mine, given to me by a very dear friend. A boyfriend, you might say. I don't skate home because of all the potholes and the traffic and the wild, wicked drivers."

"Uncle Hank," I bragged, "is a safe driver. He has balance. You don't live in Hoboken, do you?"

"My stars, no! Right here in Manhattan, downtown on Laight Street. I don't suppose you gentlemen know where Laight Street is."

"Uncle Hank can tell me and I'll navigate. Do you ever take a cab home?"

"Not if I can help it." Her eyes had gone back to being light blue. "Those cabbies are devils behind the wheel. No, I'll take the subway any day."

"Not today you won't," said Uncle Hank. "Today you'll take a yellow taxicab."

"But I can't afford one." She smiled, understanding us perfectly.

"You can afford one today," I said. Like some old guy in a movie, I rose and helped her up after me. "Today the meter won't click once."

We skated to the rental shop in the middle of the

park. Uncle Hank paid for his skates and mine while Marcella pulled on a pair of black-button boots. Then we walked back to the taxi.

"Girlfriends are funny to try finding," said Marcella. "The harder you look, the better they hide. Only when you forget to look do they leap out at you. Isn't that your experience, Pilot Hank?"

"Indeed it is."

"Of course, witches have it easy in the romance department. Witches and piano players. You don't play piano, Pilot?"

"No." He unlocked the cab door. "Not a note." Marcella waited until I was seated on my phone books, then followed me in. I sat between her and Uncle Hank in the front seat.

"If you don't play," she told him, "I'll have to teach you. First we'll see how you drive, and how your assistant navigates. Most cabbies haven't a notion where Laight Street might be. But then, most cabbies don't have such smart helpers."

"That's for sure." Uncle Hank buckled his seat belt and watched to see that we did the same. "Pilot to Navigator."

"Come in, Pilot. Time to set our course?"

"Roger. Perhaps down the West Side Highway to Vestry, then around the usual way onto Laight—?"

"Just what I was thinking, Pilot, unless the passenger has some other idea."

Marcella patted my cheek with a hand that wasn't at all scaly, but soothing and warm. "The passenger approves of everything. South to Tribeca, dear Navigator, and I'll show you how a piano should sound, and how a crumb cake should taste, and maybe a thing or two more."

3
Miss Ruby

There was a single lock on Marcella's door, not three like at our house in Brooklyn. And when we arrived, the one lock wasn't latched. But this seemed no surprise to Marcella.

"You've been robbed!" I said hopefully. "Don't go in till I've checked for footprints."

"Nonsense, Kid Crime. I've had a visit from Miss Ruby who lives upstairs. At her age she's forgetful and leaves the door open, but I don't mind. She's a neighbor, and a home is no good without neighbors. Isn't that so?"

"I'm not sure." As many years as I had lived on Clinton Street in Brooklyn, I wondered who my neighbors might be. Also I wondered where the crumb cake might be hidden. It's possible to wonder many things at the same time, because I *also* wondered if only old ladies lived in this place, since it was so creaky and cramped and full of dark corners—just the sort of place where old ladies would live. It was easy picturing Marcella's neighbor Miss Ruby: tall and bony, with trembling hands and a drooling stinky mouth . . .

I peered through the doorway. "Marcella, are you the only witch here, or is this house full of—"

"*Full* of us, of course it is!" She laughed so the gap showed in the front of her mouth. "Where else could I live? You know how hard it is to find a good home in New York, a likable place you can afford—"

I nodded. Apartments and co-ops, condos and brownstones, were all my parents' friends talked about.

"Well, then! I looked and looked, and when I found this house I had to snap it up, such a perfect hideaway for witches, so tiny, so long and crooked. But only *nice* witches, except maybe Ruby, who wears too much red and has a mean streak. But I suppose at her age it's excusable. Come in now, come *in,* or you'll let in the rats." She held the door open.

I did go in, but slowly. Until Marcella turned on the light the hallway was dark, and I didn't move for fear of squashing spiders and snakes and slime. But when the light popped on there was nothing creepy to be seen. In fact, the hallway, lined high with books, opened onto a room quite airy and bright. But it was daytime. "Marcella, you don't have—ghosts here, do you?"

"No," she sighed, "not often. Only at midnight, and then only when the moon is full. Once a month if we're lucky."

"Lucky?" I sat down in a rocking chair that was so perfectly my size, it might have been waiting for me. Uncle Hank squawked at a stuffed bird mounted in a cage beside the front window. He looked silly talking to a bird that was so bright blue and green that it couldn't possibly be real. "You feel *lucky* to be haunted?"

"Oh, yes. Our ghost is my grandmother, I wouldn't part with her for anything. She wears loose light veils and sometimes plays the flute, and she bakes the best crumb cake—"

"Crumb cake," I repeated, as if I could taste the cake just by saying the words. "Crumb cake."

And as I said it again, the stuffed bird cackled, "Crumb cake! Crumb cake! Wanta piece a crumb cake!" and frantically fluffed her wings. I nearly rocked out of the rocking chair and onto the floor.

"Gracious me." Marcella smiled. "Kyle, Kyle—so stirred up at the mention of food! You aren't hungry, by any chance?"

"Yes," I said weakly, eyes fixed on the bird. "Hungry."

Uncle Hank scratched his beard. "I don't know if we should eat cake that's contaminated."

"Contami—what, Uncle?"

"I mean baked by a ghost. Haunted crumb cake. You think it's safe, Kid?"

"Crumb cake! Crumb cake!" cried the bird, rocking the cage sideways and throwing sparkles of sunlight across the room. "Wanta piece a *crumb* cake!" she screamed, so loudly that Uncle Hank clapped his hands over his ears.

"Ophelia doesn't care for crackers." Marcella shrugged. "But she adores cake. We could let her come out and have some—"

"Wait," I called, to stop Uncle Hank from opening the cage. "Will she bite us?"

"She's usually not too vicious, though one time she did take a nip from a schoolboy's ear. Still, she didn't harm his other one, so it might have been worse. From living with witches, Ophelia prefers the company of girls—but she won't bite if you treat her kindly. Like females of any species, she responds well to affection."

"Oh," said Uncle Hank, "I've known a few who didn't."

Marcella smiled as Uncle carefully opened the cage. With a great rustling and fluttering, the bird flew across the room and onto Marcella's wrist.

"*I* know, Uncle. We'll give her a piece of cake, and then—then we'll *watch* her."

"And so? What will *watching* her show?"

"It'll show if the ghost cake does something bad to her. If she doesn't die, we can eat."

"Kid Kyle, you're a scientist. All right, let's give Ophelia some cake."

When Marcella held a piece in her hand, Ophelia pecked and pecked with her hooked yellow beak. Finished, she cocked her head to the side and let loose an impressive burp.

"Very good," said Marcella, when we had stopped laughing. "Very good, Ophelia. And now—"

"Very good!" shrieked the bird. "Very good, very good!"

"And *now,*" said Marcella, like a mother at bedtime, "go back to your cage, Ophelia. Back to your cage."

Ophelia tilted her head one way, then tilted the other, then called, "Back to your cage! Back to your cage!"

Marcella placed a chunk of cake on the cage's top shelf. "Back to your cage," she snapped, in a voice that a bird—or a ghost, or anyone—would certainly understand. Ophelia flew inside and pecked at the cake.

Marcella was closing the gold door when there echoed, from some other corner of the room, a thin gruff voice much like the bird's voice but also much different. "Back to your cage!" it whispered hoarsely. "Back to your cage!"

"So." Marcella smiled without turning her head. "It's you, is it, Ruby?"

Pressed into my chair so far I could press no farther, I searched for the tall skinny witch. At first I missed her. She stood quite still, and wasn't tall or old but a tiny red scowl of a girl. She stepped out from the hallway, her dress dark red, her sneakers dark red, her black eyes trained on mine. "Back to your cage," she hissed, "and *maybe* I'll give you some cake."

"That's enough, Ruby. We won't have you scaring our company." Marcella spoke calmly, as if her heart were not frozen like mine.

"He isn't *my* company." For just an instant, Ruby seemed to regret I wasn't her company. "I don't *like* boys." Her hair hung straight and smooth and as black as a black cat's fur—and her eyes, if anything, shone blacker. Even her skin glowed deeply, deeply tan. "Ophelia is *my* parrot." She glared away from me to the cage. "Phooey-phooey!"

"Phooey-phooey!" hooted the bird, her voice so like Ruby's that it made my head buzz.

Ruby was teeny, yet acted so big that I couldn't help asking, "How old are you, Ruby?"

"Seven years old and I hate boys."

"Then we're even, because I hate girls."

"Bully for you! Now I want cake."

"We all want cake," purred Marcella. "Don't we, Kid Kyle?"

"Only if it isn't haunted. Did Ruby make it?"

"No, Honey."

"And it's not haunted!" Ruby, even on tiptoes, stood as high as I sat in the chair. "It's not haunted, it's only crumb cake."

"Crumb cake!" echoed the parrot. "Crumb cake!" We all laughed, even Ruby. Then we headed into the kitchen to eat.

"But Marcella," I said when I finished my milk. "You didn't play the piano! You were going to show Uncle Hank—"

"Child, you and this red whip have worn me out. I'll play some tunes next time."

"You're inviting us back?"

"Indeed I am. This house could use some—"

"Marcella." Ruby stared at the table. "Are you sure?"

"Never surer. They're invited back any Sunday they'd like to come. The Pilot, the Navigator, and the good ship *Happenchance.*"

"And what is that supposed to mean?"

"It *means,* Sweetness, that these two men are the crew of a taxi-ship. If I were you, I'd show some respect."

"Well." Ruby crossed her arms like the sort of grown-up who wants to be serious but doesn't know what to say. "I'll give this some thought."

We were safe in the cab, rolling back toward Brooklyn, when Uncle Hank finally spoke. "So—would you like to go straight home, or would you rather drive awhile?"

"Rather drive," I said. "Anywhere."

"I know how you feel. I suppose you'd rather not talk about that pest Ruby—?"

"No," I barked. "Rather not."

"She liked you, you know. I could tell."

"Did *not.*" I felt bad for sounding so cross, but I couldn't help myself. "Anyhow, I didn't like *her,* the little brat. Let's just drive and not talk, okay, Uncle?"

"Sure." I thought I'd hurt his feelings—but when I looked across, my uncle was smiling. "Kid Kyle, we should go back there sometime, since old Marcella invited us. You liked *her,* didn't you?"

"She's all right. I guess we can go back if you want, Uncle—just to be polite."

The trees in Battery Park were yellow and red, and the air coming in my window tasted deliciously clean, and I didn't know if I was happy or dizzy or angry or what.

4
Down from the Tower

My parents must have decided to trust Uncle Hank, because they let us drive together often now; we were a Sunday team.

One week we finally visited the Museum of Natural History, like we had tried doing months earlier on the day of the Hoboken Watch. This time we reached the museum without any hassle and roamed through dozens of rooms that showed deep-window displays called dioramas. I decided dioramas were interesting—at least interesting enough to tell Mom about later, when I'd have to tell her that *something* was interesting. My problem with the dioramas was that they showed all these wild animals—like zebras, ostriches, and rhinos—which everyone knew had been dead for years, and they were mounted in fancy round backgrounds that were supposed to look alive but didn't look alive really. They were interesting, like I told Uncle Hank—but not really *cool.*

According to Hoboken Time, we were in the museum for over an hour. Seventy-four minutes. Then, outside, we saw a man dressed in black who juggled torches and swallowed their flames. We watched him for only eighteen minutes, but I told Uncle Hank I thought he was the most interesting thing all afternoon, because he was alive. He wasn't behind glass or anything else—I could feel the heat from his flames.

Back in the taxi, we fastened our seat belts and headed down Columbus Avenue. From our car we watched sidewalk clowns who rode unicycles, fiddlers who fiddled in top hats, and a pale skinny man who had his arm in the air.

"Should we take him, Uncle?"

"Only if you run the meter and make change."

We stopped and the man climbed in.

He slipped a pair of dark glasses onto his nose. "Take me to Nomo," he breathed, his voice silky. "Downtown, way downtown. Under the Beach and over the Frank. No of the Mo." He seemed to be staring at me through his sunglasses, but I couldn't be sure. Uncle Hank drove us down Broadway until it turned into Seventh, then on down Seventh through the Village. From time to time he checked Mister Nomo in his mirror. "You mean North Moore," he said finally.

"You got it, my man. Crib 76. Hang a Ralph past the fuzz-box." And the man giggled, as if he thought he was on TV.

I kept close track of our route. As Uncle Hank liked to say, the navigator should study every new route so he'll know it the next time. Seventh became Varick. We waited for the light at Canal, crossed, passed a police station, and turned right. A block later Uncle Hank stopped at number 76, and I pressed the meter button.

"That's six-twenty-five," I said. "Plus the tip, if you think we—"

"No tip, no tip." The man stood outside. "That's only for the ones who know."

"Who know what, Mister?"

He trained his dark glasses on us. "I, you see, am a poet. And a painter and a musician. And my tip for you—"

"We can do without your tip," Uncle Hank said, and drove us quickly away. We rolled west on Nomo.

"Was he crazy, Uncle?"

"Sometimes it's hard to be sure. But he certainly was a New York talker. There's plenty of talk in New York. People in shades trying to impress other people in shades."

"But you don't wear shades, Uncle." He had explained to me once before that shades were really sunglasses.

"Not anymore." From West Street we took a right on Vestry. "But forget that guy, Kyle. Let's have a geography quiz. Do you know where we are?"

"Yes," I groaned, checking to be sure the brown metal awning still stuck out at the corner where we should turn onto Laight Street. "This is Ruby's—I mean Marcella's—block. There, around the next corner." The pair of round wooden water tanks on the roof across the street hadn't changed either.

"You're a born navigator. This *is* their block, and this is our day for a visit."

"If you say so." I was glad he had made the decision for me.

"I like visiting these witches," said Uncle Hank. I could tell, even without looking, that he was smiling. "But I'm not so sure your mom and dad would be enthusiastic. You know what I mean? They might think such witches were a little, well—"

"A little weird."

"Right." Uncle Hank grinned at me. "So maybe we should keep this visit to ourselves, you know what I mean?"

"Sure, Uncle."

We parked in front of the tiny house. I stood behind him while he rang the bell.

Finally Ruby arrived to open the door.

"Oh, it's *you.*" She wrinkled her nose at Uncle Hank and gave no sign of noticing me. "Come in, then— don't stand there." She turned and skipped up the steps, her red dress whirling from sight.

Marcella's door stood open; she sat at the piano tracing a melody with one finger. "Warlock Kyle! And Pilot Hank!" She rose and gave us each a strong kiss on the cheek. "We knew you'd be stopping today—"

"Who knew?" I asked, as if I didn't actually care.

"Miss Ruby and I. Not more than an hour ago, she said, 'They won't be much longer, I can feel it.' "

"Never!" came a shrill voice from the hallway or the closet or somewhere. "Never ever!"

"We might have been earlier," I bragged, "but we were riding around Manhattan in the taxi. First we went to a museum to learn things, and then we saw a man eat fire, and then we brought a weird guy downtown, to Nomo Street, and he wore dark glasses and was a painter and a musician and—what else was he, Uncle?"

"A poet."

"That's right," I nodded. "A poet."

"He was not!" glared Ruby, stepping out from behind the ferns. "He wasn't anything!"

"You may be right," smiled Uncle Hank. "I'm guessing he was a talker."

"Only a *talker,* yes. Like—like—*Kyle.* Only a talker." Ruby tapped one red sneaker up and down. "Anyway, what was the name of his street?"

"Nomo." I wondered when she would sting. "But that's just what *he* called it. Really it's North Moore Street, right, Uncle?"

"Yes. And some people call it Nathaniel Moore Street. But the street sign only says N. Moore. What do you witches call it, Miss Ruby?"

"We call it Nathaniel, of course—Nathaniel, ah, Moore, like you said. North Moore is all wrong."

"Witches know some things," I snorted, "but cab-drivers know streets. Anyhow, I'm not sure you *are* a witch."

This only put a meaner gleam in Ruby's eye. She ran to the front window and whispered to Ophelia the parrot, who had been sitting peaceably on her perch. We all stood listening, but nothing happened. Ruby whispered again. Ophelia tilted her head, fluffed her feathers, and shrieked, "Kyle's a creep, Kyle's a creep!" with all her force.

The room fell very quiet. Ruby approached me, her cheeks flushed. "Now do you dare say I'm not a witch?"

I didn't say *anything,* because I was about to cry. But I would *not* cry in front of Ruby. And I wouldn't cry in front of Uncle Hank, because he was my pilot and I was his navigator, and crew members, like cowboys, don't cry in front of each other. Then I felt Marcella's hand on mine. She led me into the hallway, saying something about showing me the roof.

"It's *my* roof!" wailed Ruby.

There was steel in Marcella's voice. "The roof belongs to all of us equally, and now Kyle and I are going up there. By ourselves. Ruby, you *can* be a witch, a spiteful little witch I shouldn't share my secrets with."

Ruby gasped. "You'll tell *him* a secret you won't tell *me?*"

"Worse than that, Precious. I might tell him a secret *about* you. You can be naughty—that's your privilege and I won't stop you—but you must accept the consequences of your naughtiness. Don't look so ignorant, child, I've explained this often enough before. Entertain Pilot Hank, now—we won't be long."

Marcella was closing the door behind us when Ruby thrust herself in the way. "Marcella?" she whimpered. "*Please,* Marcella, don't show him the roof?" She seemed so close to tears herself that I felt mine go dry from astonishment. "Please, Marcella?"

"Honey, don't be tragic. But the truth is, daytime isn't best for showing off the roof. It looks much more wondrous at night. So I have an offer for you. I won't show Kyle the roof today, but only if you agree to show it to him yourself, later, when he's here after dark. Do you accept my offer?"

"Maybe."

"Do you *accept?*"

"Okay. I'll show him." Ruby let out a breath three times her size. "But not today. Are you still going to tell him a secret?"

"Nothing that will hurt you, I swear. Go on in now and grant us some peace. We may go upstairs to the landing, but we won't go on the roof."

Ruby stomped inside. We heard her calling "phooey-phooey" to the parrot, and the parrot calling back, as we climbed to the top of the steps. Marcella sat on the landing close beside me. "Just wait a second," she huffed, "until I get my breath back. These stairs seem higher each time I climb them."

I waited.

"There, I feel better. And do *you* feel any better now, Kid Navigator?"

"Lots. Why does Ruby hate me so much?"

"No, she doesn't hate you, and that's what the secret is about. It has to do with the parrot Ophelia, but mostly it has to do with Miss Ruby."

"Even Ophelia hates me. Did you hear what she screamed?"

"We all heard. But that bird doesn't know the meaning of what she says. She knows only how to repeat sounds. Someone has to teach her what to say, by hanging a cloth over her cage and repeating the same words, time after time after time, with great care, until Ophelia learns to repeat them."

“ ‘Kyle’s a creep, Kyle’s a creep.’ ”

“Yes. An awful thing to teach her. And who did the teaching?”

“Ruby, of course. Because she hates me.”

“Ruby. Yes. But not because she hates you. To the contrary—she did it because she’s afraid to say she likes you.”

“Uncle Hank said that, too. I mean, that Ruby likes me. But he was wrong and so are you.”

Marcella chuckled, making a whistling noise where her front tooth should have been. “Your uncle is an observant man. Well, that’s the secret. Ruby would say she hated me if she knew I had told you, but she wouldn’t hate me really, because she’d have told you herself if she weren’t so proud and so—scared.”

“She doesn’t seem scared to me.”

“We’re all scared sometimes. Even a witch. Even a taxi driver. Hasn’t your uncle told you?”

“Only that he’s scared some nights in his cab when he feels all alone—”

“See what I mean? Let’s go downstairs now and deal with the demon.”

We had gone down one or two steps when a door opened beside us and a beautiful woman came out, a woman who could only have been Ruby’s mother. She wore a baggy white shirt spotted with paint, and her skin was even more deeply tan than Ruby’s, and her eyes were just as black, but prettier, because they knew how to smile.

"You must be Kyle, the taxi-boy." She spoke with a soft strange accent that made her more beautiful still. "I've heard about you time and again these past days. You've created quite a stir in this house. My name is Lydia." She shook my hand as if I were a grown-up.

"You're Ruby's mother," I stammered.

"Yes."

"And are you—" I faltered, not believing it possible. "Are you a witch, too?"

Lydia glanced at Marcella. "Not much of one. You'll have to judge for yourself."

"Enough of this stalling," Marcella broke in. "Are you ready to come down with us, Lydia, and meet your destiny?"

I had no idea what Marcella meant. But I began to understand when we entered her front room, and Uncle Hank saw Ruby's mother and an incredible change came over his face. His mouth dropped partway open, then closed tightly as he tried looking anywhere but at Lydia. She also seemed like she couldn't speak, and Marcella was no help. Finally I had to say something. "Uncle, this is Lydia, Ruby's mom. And this is my uncle Hank, Mrs. Lydia. He drives a taxi and goes everywhere."

Before either could speak, Ruby stamped her red

foot for attention. She peered hard into my eyes, as if to discover the secret I'd learned. "Don't call her Mrs. Lydia, Kyle. We call her Lydia, just Lydia."

"Fine." I couldn't figure why Ruby no longer looked angry. "And what do you call your dad?"

"Don't have one."

"You mean he doesn't live here?" Lots of my classmates had fathers who lived somewhere else.

"No," Ruby insisted. "I don't *have* one. He pushed Lydia off the castle, and that was when he stopped being my father. Even before I was born," she added, to increase my confusion. "Right, Lydia?"

"Yes, Darling." Lydia smiled sadly as she spoke. "That was when he ceased to be your father, when I was in the air. Even before I landed."

"So really he wasn't my father at all, was he?"

"No, Darling. He's never seen you and he never will."

"A castle?" I repeated. "You fell off a castle and—into the air?"

"Yes." Lydia's mind seemed far away until she sighed half a smile and explained. "It was in Germany, way across the ocean from here."

"Did you fall—far?"

"From the top of the castle's highest tower. Such a long time ago. There was a balcony at the top of the tower, with a wooden railing, and when he pushed me, the railing broke."

"And *then,*" said Ruby, "when the Rich Man pushed her—we call him the Rich Man, not my father—Lydia fell off the castle and into the sky."

"All the way to the—?"

"All the way," said Lydia in her soft foreign voice. "Far enough to think about dying, and to see the river rush up at me."

I thought of Dad pushing Mom from the top of a castle. "But how *far* did you fall? Farther than from the top of this house?"

"Oh, yes," said Lydia, her smile full of sorrow. "It was as far, they told me later, as from the highest branch of the highest tree."

"But how could the Rich Man do that to you?"

"We fought all the time, Kyle. Before we married, after we married—he loved to scream and I screamed back, silently, in my own way. But that was our last fight, when he tested my wings."

If Ruby had been the one telling me, or even Marcella, I might not have believed a word. But Lydia's eyes were as steady and calm as her voice.

"Weren't you even *hurt?*"

"Oh, yes, terribly. How could I not be, after dropping down and down into that river? Even water can be hard to land on when you fall from high enough in the sky." Her eyes met mine and I had to look away from their pain. "Certainly I was hurt. Both my legs were broken and one of my arms, and my insides were all stirred around. But not my baby. I've always known it was Ruby who saved me."

"You were—" At first I couldn't remember the word. "You were *pregnant?*"

"Yes, but I didn't know it yet, and I never did tell the brute who—well, the Rich Man. Ruby was no more than a speck at the time, and she wasn't born until eight months later, when I was all back together."

"Better than Humpty Dumpty," I said, and everyone smiled.

"Ruby guided me down to the river and away from that man. You see, Kyle, he was so rich he owned the castle. He had bought it only the day before, a miraculous misty day, a day when nothing seemed quite real and I felt I still loved him. But that morning, when we stood at the top of the tower, the river mist burned off—and far, far away in the distance, he saw another castle looming high over the river, higher even than *his* castle. He was a strange man, rather like these men in New York City, each wanting to own a building higher than all the others—and he had to have the very highest and grandest castle on the river. When he saw that other castle in the distance, he seemed to lose his mind."

"He went crazy?"

"In a way, yes. It was as if nothing around him was good enough—not his new castle, not me, nothing. And I was closest, I was easiest to break. He started shouting, and I shouted silently back, and he pushed me off the tower." Lydia turned to Ruby. "Don't ever marry a rich man, Darling."

"I won't marry anybody. Boys are mean and I hate them."

"Yes, yes," said Marcella. "And I suppose *you* are *not* mean, Miss Sunshine? You, who flew before you were born?"

"I'm the meanest." Ruby smiled the smile of a red angel. "Would you like to hear a secret, Kyle?"

"I already heard one from Marcella."

"Bully for you—I heard one from your uncle! Do you want to hear another or not?"

"Yes," I said. "Please."

"You others," Ruby ordered, "go into the kitchen. Go talk or brew tea or something. We need our privacy."

"At your command." Marcella led Uncle Hank and Lydia down the hall.

Ruby made sure the kitchen door had closed, then turned to face me. "Do you promise not to tell? I can't share it unless you promise."

"All right, I promise."

"Well! It's something I couldn't say in front of Lydia, because it would embarrass her." Ruby leaned toward me as if we were old friends. "But the truth is, she limps."

"She wasn't limping a minute ago. Anyway, she isn't *that* old—why should she limp?"

"From the fall, stupid! From being pushed off the castle! You have to watch hard, but then you'll see, specially in cold weather or when it rains. But she doesn't want anyone to know, so you won't tell, will you?"

"Not even Uncle Hank."

"Good. Now give *me* a secret."

"Okay." At first I couldn't find one. I thought about school, and my parents, and Uncle Hank—as soon as I thought of him, I knew he had to be at the center of the secret. "Let's see," I told Ruby. "My uncle Hank is a cabdriver. But you know that already."

"Go on—what's the secret?"

"Don't know yet. I'm looking for it."

"Here, I'll tell you another one while you look for yours. We have a secret key to our house."

"You mean Marcella carries it?"

"I mean we *hide* it, it's our secret. A gold key that we buried in the flowerpot outside the house—the third flowerpot from the left. Or maybe from the right. No, the *left*. And no one knows about it but us witches. And now you, of course, since I told you."

"We don't have any hidden keys at our house." I was full of admiration.

"Doesn't matter. So, have you found your secret yet? Tell me while you look—I love puzzles."

"Well, it has something to do with last year and the

year before, when Uncle Hank went traveling. In Europe and Greece and the top of Africa—"

"In Morocco?" asked Ruby.

"How did *you* know?"

"I guess things lucky sometimes. Marcella says I have powers. But I didn't really guess Morocco, it's the only place I know in Africa. Lydia was born there. She was a baby there like I was a baby in France. And then, when she was little, her parents took her to England, just like she brought me to New York when *I* was little."

"Lydia was born in Morocco? Then that's why her skin is so dark, and her eyes—"

"Yes, Kyle—dark like mine."

We huddled together, our faces close, and I knew we had almost reached the secret—and then I realized that it wasn't only about Uncle Hank, it was about Lydia too, and yes, it was about me, in a way, because I had seen it myself—

"Now I have it, Ruby!"

"Yes?" She leaned so close to my face, I was scared she'd try kissing me.

"Uncle Hank sent me postcards of all the places he saw, but he didn't say how he was traveling. I thought he was in a taxi, since here in New York he was always in a taxi."

"That's the secret?" Ruby's lips drooped.

"No, no, no! The secret is that in my mind I saw

him going in a yellow cab across the desert. And I saw a woman who sat beside him. A beautiful dark woman—"

"—And she had dark eyes? And straight black hair, like Lydia's—?"

"Yes! It was Lydia I saw, but Uncle Hank didn't see her, he didn't find her in Morocco because she wasn't *there* anymore. And that's why he looked so sad when he came back to New York."

"He won't look sad now, and neither will Lydia. But are you positive it was her you saw?"

"Had to be. Still, we can check. We just have to get her into the taxi beside Uncle Hank, the way I saw them in my head."

"That's easy. Wait and see—she's a fool for ice cream."

In the kitchen the grown-ups didn't seem as happy as we were. Marcella said nothing; Uncle Hank and Lydia watched the tea leaves swirl in their cups. Ruby broke the silence.

"Kyle says he drives around in a taxi, but I don't believe him. I think he takes the bus and *says* he drives in a taxi. He says he can prove it—his uncle will drive us all to Chinatown for ice cream."

Ruby waited for the laughter to stop, and then continued, sounding very much like a teacher. "There's one rule you all have to follow, which is that Pilot Hank and Lydia sit in the front seat, and the rest of us sit in back."

"But why?" smiled her mother.

"Lydia, it's the rule, and if you want ice cream you'll have to follow it. Now! Is everyone ready?"

"I'm ready," said Uncle Hank. "And Kid Kyle looks ready. And the ice cream will be free, paid for by the poet of Nomo Street."

So off we went, with Lydia sitting in front. And once I saw her there, I had no doubt that she *was* the dark woman of the desert. When I whispered the good news to Ruby, she tilted her head like a parrot and grinned all the way to the ice cream store.

5

When Good News Isn't

It happened in the middle of October.

The lawyers at Dad's office held a meeting—I mean, the lawyers who were already partners, like Dad wanted to be. They met, and they decided who would become a new partner and who wouldn't, and they didn't choose Dad.

When he came home that night I couldn't tell if he was very angry or just very tired, because he didn't say anything. He sat and drank one martini after another and stared at the TV—which didn't make sense, because the TV wasn't even turned on.

Finally Mom said to him, "There's always next year, Darling. They'll vote again next year—"

"But not for me. If they don't like me now, they won't like me then. It's finished. Six years of slavery for nothing. Some law firm, hey? Snorkel, Bork, and Boom. Finished."

"But it isn't the end of the world. You can work for another firm, maybe a smaller one that's more fun—"

"More fun," said Dad. "Right. More fun. I quit."

He was still staring at the TV, and it was still off, so I went across and turned it on to give him something to watch. If I could find a football game, it might relax him. He liked football—

"Turn that thing off."

I turned it off. "But wouldn't you like a football game, Dad? Or hockey, or—"

"Sick of football." His eyes were stranger than when he was just drunk. "Sick of the whole shebang. Sick of martinis." He scowled at the glass in his hand. Maybe he was sick of martinis, but he drank the rest anyway.

"Kyle," Mom told me, "you'd better go to bed now. You can play there till I come tuck you in."

"But it's only seven-thirty." I pointed at my Hoboken watch.

"Please, Kyle. Not tonight." She took my hand and led me from the room.

We were nearly at the door when we heard Dad say the worst thing of all. "Sick of that kid," he said to no one, since Mom was with me in the hallway.

She dropped to her knees and hugged me, but still we could hear Dad muttering.

"Sick of that kid, sick of the whole works. I quit."

"He doesn't mean it." Mom closed my door behind us. "He's very upset over what they did to him at work."

"Will he—quit, like he says?"

"Let's wait and see, Kyle. This is a very bad time for your father. I don't know what he'll do. Try to sleep," she said. Then she left me alone.

I did try. But, as Uncle Hank used to say, sleep is like the subway—it doesn't come when you want it, but only when it's ready. I wished it would arrive and carry me someplace, anyplace where no one was sick of me, but it didn't come.

I hid under the blankets and tried being an explorer in a desert tent, under a night filled with stars, where I could hear the voice of a dark princess dressed in red and the scuffling of magic camels who had three humps . . . but even through the tent and the desert and the bright starry night, I heard the echo of my father's voice.

He didn't quit his job. He drifted through the next few days, and into the next week—which was when the news came that should have been good news but wasn't.

I knew something was different when Dad got home from his job before Mom did from hers. He and I sat facing each other in the living room, in silence. Those days Dad was silent whatever he did, and I tried being silent with him.

But finally he seemed too far away. "Dad," I said.

He didn't answer.

"Dad, I want to show you something. A drawing I made in school of one of those pink monsters—"

"Not now, Kyle."

"—You know, those cross-eyed monsters with the flying hair, the kind you used to like—"

"No. Not now." He didn't look at me.

Watching him now, I remembered times when we used to admire my drawings together. Other times, Dad even drew with me, coloring goofy monsters that made me laugh. But remembering such times didn't make me laugh now.

He didn't look at his martini, he just reached inside the glass and squeezed the olive until it squished between his fingers. I stopped talking.

When Mom finally came home from the bank, it was late. Dad had drunk his first three martinis and was pouring his fourth.

"Pour one for me," she said. This was very unusual, since Mom usually drank a glass of wine, never a martini. I watched her and Dad watched her; she watched the olive in her glass. Then she looked up at Dad. "It was a strange day at work. No one would talk to me. Then at five o'clock Boss Jones said I should leave my accounts—he was taking me out for a drink. We went, and he clinked my glass, and he said—"

"He said," Dad interrupted, "that they're making you a vice president."

"Yes." Mom tried to smile. "But how could you know?"

"From the look on your face when you came in the door." He reached into his glass and pulled out a shiny wet olive and looked at it like he had never seen one before. It was the strangest thing, because I knew what he was going to do even before he did it. He stared at the shiny red and green olive for a long time while Mom and I watched him—and then he squeezed it slowly between his thumb and his fingers, crushing it, making the green and red bits squeeze out and fall back into his martini.

Mom could hardly speak. "Yes. Vice president. Aren't you going to congratulate me?"

"Cheers." Very slowly, Dad raised his glass. "Congratulations." But instead of clinking glasses as Boss Jones had done, he knocked the glass from Mom's hand, spraying martini all across the coffee table. "So you'll have your own office with your own name on the door, and you'll make fifteen grand more than me. Felicitations." Very carefully he refilled his glass from the martini pitcher.

"George," my mom said. Her voice was shaking.

But Dad didn't say anything. He stood up, slowly, balancing his glass so it wouldn't spill. He smiled very sadly down into his martini.

"George," Mom said again.

But he didn't look at her. He staggered toward the stairs, started climbing, and never stopped looking at his delicate glass full of martini and olive bits.

"Come back here!" shouted Mom. "Don't run away from this one! Come here!" She smashed her glass into the fireplace—and that moment, when her glass flew into a zillion pieces, was when everything became an awful dream. And like all the times before, I tried to stop watching but couldn't.

Slowly, slowly, Dad turned back down the stairs. His voice was low. "Don't you ever, *ever,* order me around like that."

"Come back—" she said, but before she could finish, he took two steps closer, then another step—all very slowly—and when he slapped her face, it sounded so loud to me that I was sure I felt it sting my own face across the room.

Then he shouted bad things, and she shouted worse things, with words I'd have been spanked for using. Crouching in the corner, I hugged my knees and tried not to listen. Then Mom grabbed her purse and grabbed me and pulled me out the front door. It slammed behind us.

We stood on Clinton Street, both crying like three-year-olds, and it was a miracle any cab stopped for us, because we must have looked crazy.

"Manhattan," Mom told the driver, a huge black man with a kind face. "Take us to Manhattan, to—to—the Village. Greenwich Avenue. We'll stay with Susan."

"Who's Susan, Mom?"

"My friend from work. We'll stay at her place tonight."

"Are you and Dad getting divorced, Mom?"

"Oh, I don't know. I don't know anything right now. Maybe we'll feel better tomorrow."

When we reached her friend Susan's building, Mom rang and rang but there was no answer. Then we stood outside shivering, too cold to cry.

"Where can we go, Kyle? Looking like this, I'd be ashamed to be seen anywhere else. Where can we *go?*"

She pleaded like such a kindergartner that I had to give her a serious parent-type answer. "We can go to Marcella's house. We'll be safe and snug there."

"And who is Marcella?" Mom almost smiled. "One of your little girlfriends from school?"

"Not little." At home I had never mentioned Marcella or Ruby or Lydia. "She's tall and old—*much* older than you. Her hair is white and her front tooth is gone. But she's nice, and she has a parrot named Ophelia who looks dead but is really alive. You'll like Marcella, I know you will. She told me to stop by anytime."

"And where did you meet this white-haired saint?"

"In the park, with Uncle Hank. We were skating and so was she. She wears purple." Just like a man, I stepped to the curb, hailed a cab, and let Mom climb in first. Then I helped the driver navigate, because he was new and had never heard of Laight Street. First I said to take the West Side Highway, but he didn't know how to get onto it from where we were, so I told him to try Seventh and Varick, then across Canal to Nomo, and he missed the joke but it was all right, I showed him where to turn.

Marcella's light was on, but she didn't answer the bell. Mom stayed in the cab, since Laight Street was dark and was the kind of place she called a perfect breeding ground for muggers.

"Come on back, Kyle. We'll go find a hotel."

"The lights are on upstairs. Lydia must be home."

"Lydia? Do you know everyone in this house?"

"Just about." I didn't mention the ghost. "They usually come to the door—"

Then I remembered Ruby bragging about the emergency key, hidden on the window ledge in the third flowerpot from the left. I stretched high enough to reach over its rim, then dug my fingers into the dirt.

"Come back to the cab," shouted Mom. "We'll go uptown to a good hotel."

The driver looked pleased at the chance to haul us clear to midtown and flashed me a big smile—but at that same second, my fingers felt something metal buried in the dirt. I gave a tug and the key glittered gold under the streetlight.

"Kyle, put that back! We'll be arrested!"

"They're my friends, Mom. They don't mind."

The key slipped into the lock, and turned, and the door swung open, creaking exactly as the door to a witch's house should creak. But of course I said nothing about witches. Mom was scared enough already.

"Please," she asked the driver, "will you wait until we're sure someone is here?"

"You pay now," said the man.

"Certainly. But then will you wait until we're inside?"

"No problem, Missus. You pay now five dollars fifty, please."

"Here's six," said Mom. She got out and closed the door and was amazed when the cab wheeled around the corner. "Well, that fink. He said he would wait."

"You only tipped him fifty cents, Mom. He was mad."

"But even so." Glancing down the street as if expecting a murderer to leap from the shadows, Mom hurried me inside and bolted the door behind us.

I peeked into Marcella's front room, then tugged Mom up the stairs to Ruby's floor.

Lydia opened after my third knock. "Why, Kyle!" She pulled the door wide. "How late you do ramble for a nine-year-old! And this is your mother?"

"Yes," I said grandly. "Mom, this is Lydia, Ruby's mom, but Ruby doesn't call her Mom, she calls her Lydia. Ruby wears red, and that's why they call her Ruby—no, it's the other way around. Anyway, she's seven. Ruby, I mean."

"I see." Mom sank into an armchair by the stove. "Please pardon our crashing in on you, Lydia. It's been a very odd day."

"Yes, it has," I agreed, not at all tired myself. "They made Mom into a vice president today, at her bank. And when she told Dad—who they *didn't* make partner where *he* works—he was half done with a pitcher of martinis, and he hit her in the face, and they called each other terrible names—"

"—And you had to leave," nodded Lydia. "Yes, it's all too clear."

"Nothing is clear to me," said Mom. "Except—except—" and now she started *really* crying, boohooing louder than any baby I ever heard, and it was awful to see because she was my mom and was supposed to help me when *I* cried.

"Don't cry—" I raised my hands and let them fall. But she couldn't hear me. The way she quivered and howled and shook, she couldn't hear anything. "Don't cry, Mom, please—"

Lydia put an arm around me. "We'll let her cry as long as she likes. I know it hurts for you to watch, Kyle, but for now crying is the best medicine your mother can have." Then Lydia sat on the arm of Mom's chair and held her as she would hold a baby, crooning "there-there" and "now-now" and other silly things girls say to babies, as if she were Mom's mother and not someone who had met her ten minutes before. At last, Mom stopped shuddering.

"We must be keeping you up, Lydia. We should go. May I use your phone—?"

"Nonsense. You'll sleep here. Marcella is staying at her boyfriend's place—you two can share her bed."

"The same boyfriend," I asked, "who gave her the roller skates?"

"No, Kyle, that was a long time ago. Anyway, she won't be home tonight. But someone else might visit—"

I wanted to ask if she meant the ghost, but stopped myself. Lydia went to the front window, gazed into the street, and smiled back at me. "Yes, there he is now. Why don't you run downstairs, Kyle, and let him in?"

In that house there was no guessing what surprise might be next. But I trusted Lydia and wasn't afraid of any visitor she invited, so I went to the door and opened it.

There stood Uncle Hank. We stared at each other.

"Nephew!" he said at last. "How on earth—?"

"Mom and Dad had a fight, so we ran away from home. On Clinton Street we hailed a cab, and then—"

"Who is *we?*"

"Me and Mom."

"But where's your dad?"

"He's still in Brooklyn. It was so awful, Uncle. He hit her in the *face,* just because they made her vice president and they didn't make him partner."

"And you saw all this?" Even though I was nine and not a little boy anymore, Uncle Hank picked me up and held me. He looked as sad as I felt.

"They called each other the worst names—and Dad was drunk, and said he was sick of me."

"He didn't." When Uncle Hank leaned his forehead against mine, I smelled the soothing taxi scent of his beard.

"*Sick* of me, he said. You can ask Mom."

"Well then, he didn't mean it. And my hunch is that tomorrow, when he's sober, he won't remember saying it. Being drunk does that to some people. Makes them into creatures they wouldn't recognize, later."

"But he said he's had enough, and he's sick of me, and he's going to quit, and—" I hugged Uncle Hank closer, and then I was crying the way my mom had been crying with Lydia.

Uncle Hank combed his fingers through my hair, over and over, until I stopped. "This is too much." The

CONN LIBRARY
Wayne State College
1111 Main Street
Wayne, NE 68787

muscles stood out on his jaw. "Too much. If Old George is in hell, he doesn't have to pull you in with him. But come on, we'll go upstairs. Your mother's up there?"

I made one last hiccup. "Ye-Yes, Uncle."

"You were smart to think of bringing her here—" Uncle Hank went silent when he saw Lydia at the top of the stairs. He lowered me to the floor.

"Have you brought me something?" She smiled. "There, all wrapped in paper?"

"Only a few flowers. One for you and one for Little Red and one for Marcella. Three tiny roses." We trudged up the stairs. "But since it's late and Ruby's probably asleep, let's give one to Kyle and one to his mother."

"You're sweet," said Lydia in her softest voice. I thought she might kiss him, so I turned my face away, and they laughed and didn't kiss and I was almost disappointed.

"But Uncle, you didn't tell me why *you're* here. You aren't in *love,* are you?"

"Just courting, Kid, don't worry."

"Courting?"

"Oh, that's a funny dance old fools like me do, usually in the springtime, sometimes in the fall. But let's go inside and face your mother."

"I heard that," said Mom from behind Lydia. Her

eyes were puffy but she tried to smile. "You have some explaining to do, Hank Paradazckl."

"As always." Uncle turned toward me and tried looking worried. "We're in trouble again, Kid. We're in the hot, hot water."

Mom shook her head. "No, this time I'm the one in trouble."

"Yeah, I hear Old George smacked you. It's kind of hard to imagine—I've never seen him smack anyone. This law firm fiasco really got to him."

"That's part of it." First Mom frowned at Uncle Hank in his blue jeans and faded sweatshirt, and then she began to laugh. "So what else have you two done on your Sunday drives? Where else have you gone?"

"Oh," he said, "a few places."

"And you have other secrets?"

"Sure, a few. Don't we, Kid?" He nodded at me and I nodded back. "A few smallish secrets. But none that would hurt anyone. Right, Kid?"

"Right."

Lydia poured out four cups of hot chocolate, and we sat and drank until suddenly, for no reason at all, I was very tired. Lydia led us down the stairs to Marcella's bed. It was so wide and safe, and so warmly filled with such unwitchlike smells, that I was asleep before Mom could climb in beside me.

6
Inside and Outside

At home on Clinton Street, the screaming and name-calling went quiet for a few days but then started again and didn't stop. And the wilder things grew in Brooklyn, the more often Uncle Hank arrived and took me out driving. He said that his nerves got as raw as mine from such a commotion—a little time away from the screamers would be good for us both.

One afternoon we cruised up First Avenue in Manhattan and scanned the sidewalks for anyone who might give us an idea of what I should be for Halloween. The streets were crowded but we didn't see anything new, just the usual tourists, plus the older kids Uncle Hank called blue-hairs and spike-heads.

"Uncle, I'm not going as a punk rocker. Every kid

who can't think of anything good will be a punk rocker."

"Right. Something will come to us if we wait." We took Thirteenth Street across to Seventh Avenue, then rattled down Seventh to Greenwich, which led us across to Eighth Street, which was where—on the corner of Fifth Avenue—we saw the woman and her little boy. Without asking, Uncle Hank knew I wanted to take them. That was what a taxi team we had become.

"Your off-duty light was on," said the woman. "I didn't think you would stop."

"We wouldn't have," I answered. "But you looked special, so we changed our minds." I got the meter clicking, then turned and asked the boy his name.

"My name's Fred and I'm four and I'm going to see my daddy!" He puffed himself up like a blond balloon. "Is that taxi-man your daddy?"

"No, he's my uncle. What street would you like, Fred?"

"My daddy's street!" He bounced up and down.

"We're going to Franklin and Church," said his mother, who didn't look nearly as happy as little Fred.

"Daddy's street," I repeated. "Then—are you divorced?"

"Fred's father and I are divorced. Yes."

I decided to cheer her up by letting her know she wasn't alone. "*My* mom and dad might get divorced. They're trying to decide right now."

"I'm sorry to hear that." From the look on her face, I saw I hadn't helped her at all.

The more I talked, the more I wished I hadn't, and the more I couldn't stop. "You see, my dad drinks too much, and last week he hit Mom, and so she took me away to Manhattan. Now we've moved back with him in Brooklyn, but all they do is shout and fight, because Mom got promoted and Dad didn't. Still, they let me drive around in the taxi more."

"That's nice," whispered Fred's mother.

When we stopped at Franklin and Church, Uncle Hank asked if she wanted us to wait and drive her home. She said no thanks, she needed to have a talk with Fred's father. She paid me, and helped smiley Fred onto the sidewalk. As they walked into the building, he looked like the little brother I might have had but didn't have, and might not have ever. We drove away.

"Does being divorced do that to everyone, Uncle?"

"Does it do what?"

"Wasn't Fred's mom about to cry?"

"Yeah, being divorced makes everyone cry, at least for a while."

We drove on in silence. And though we didn't find my Halloween face, I didn't care—the only faces I could see were the face of Fred's mother, ready to cry, and my own mother with her shiny eye all puffed shut.

We turned left on Canal and south along the Hudson River, and I knew even before Uncle Hank did it that he would make another left on Vestry.

"So," I said, "we're going to Ruby's house. Good. But really it's Marcella I want to see. A witch like her should have some ideas for Halloween."

Uncle Hank smiled. "Right. She's the one I want to see, too."

But Marcella wasn't home, so we settled for the company of Ruby and Lydia. Uncle Hank didn't seem to mind. He sat in Lydia's second floor studio and watched her paint, and closed the door, he said, so Ruby and I could have some some privacy. I wondered if he wanted some privacy himself.

Ruby and I stayed in her room—which of course was painted red—where we made a tent of her red blankets and sheets.

"There's sand *everywhere,*" she said, "except in our food."

"Yeah. And outside this little tent, tied up to a palm tree, is our big camel named Sandra."

"With saddles for both of us, right?"

"Sure. Two-saddle Sandra."

"And three humps, Sandra has?"

"That's right, because she's a magic camel. And then to protect her, on the ground, there's a great long snake—"

"Right, with four eyes."

"Four?" I waited to hear Ruby's next idea. They never stopped popping out of her.

"Two eyes in front and two in back, you know—so it can see from both its head *and* tail. And in the middle our snake has a rattle, by its long skinny stomach, so whenever it wiggles past some hidden chocolate—"

"—The rattle makes its rattly noise and tells the snake to stop and look around?"

"Right," grinned Ruby. "And you know what? I think *my* stomach is starting to rattle right now."

"And I just heard it," said Lydia, who was standing at the entrance to our tent. "May I serve you explorers some peppermint tea?"

We let her serve us, and let her explain that peppermint tea is what the tent people of Morocco drink to fight the afternoon heat. She brought us a pot with a thin gold spout and two china cups we had to fill and refill with great care. And to go with the tea, since we were on a long caravan across the widest desert in the world, Lydia brought us a plate of dark shiny things she called dates. We needed our strength, she said, if we were to reach the far side.

She asked our permission to withdraw, leaving us to sigh about heat and humidity and all the dangers faced by fearless explorers such as ourselves. We had finished the deliciously sticky dates, and were discussing whether lizards tasted better roasted or fried, when Marcella's piano began playing below us.

"Let's go hear some blues," urged Ruby. "Some low-down blues."

"Okay." We scrambled from our tent and left the desert behind, while I wondered what low-down blues might be.

Marcella nodded as we settled onto the sofa, but she didn't stop playing, her left hand marching up and down the lower keys, her right hand plinking out single melody notes and sprays of notes together, like bouquets that formed and fell apart in all different shades of sadness. I was thinking of the divorced woman in the taxi when Marcella started to sing.

> Every night, I just lie awake
> Every night, I just lie awake
> You know I call out your name
> I feel my heart will break
>
> You left me high, dry, all alone
> A boat without a paddle
> A dog without a bone—
> Oh Darling, how could you treat me so?
> You left me high and dry
> With no place to go

Then there were more single notes, and bunches of notes together, until the song ended with a handful of notes that reminded me of the tiny roses Uncle Hank had brought Lydia. Except these weren't red roses, they were miniature musical roses of such dark blue they were almost purple, like Marcella's dress. And when I saw those blue roses in my head was when I knew what Ruby had meant by the low-down blues.

Then Marcella played a slower song without words. This time the sound wasn't like flowers but more like faraway stars, bright gold and silver, calling out from deep in the sky, from a terribly lonely place. And these musical stars weren't close together but far apart, calling out across the darkest blue-black sky, each star wishing for a friend. When Marcella finished the song, she closed the lid over the piano keys and turned to face us.

"Was that all right, Kyle?"

"It was like the sky. Lonely. But the other one was so unhappy—you know, the one about her being divorced."

"Yes. About love. Does everything remind you of divorce?"

"Not everything. I just don't want Dad to throw Mom off a castle."

"None of us want that, and it won't happen. Let's go for a walk."

"To Chinatown?" suggested Ruby.

"Not ice cream. Just a walk, to see what we see."

"Before we came here, Uncle Hank drove me

around the Village, looking for what I want to be on Halloween. But we didn't find it."

"Maybe," said Marcella, "you didn't look in the right place. Maybe you should look in the river."

"I should be a *fish* for Halloween?"

"An octopus!" Ruby tickled her hands up the sides of my face. "All slimy and gooey—or an eel! Shouldn't Kyle be an eel?"

"Let's go for that walk," was all Marcella would say.

We shouted upstairs to tell the others we were going, and Lydia called back that it was okay, she and Uncle Hank would see us when we came back.

Once we were outside, Marcella moved ahead of us with sweeping purple strides; I had to walk fast to catch up, and little Ruby, in her red jeans and sweater, had to run.

"I always forget how short your legs are," said Marcella, making Ruby stick out her tongue. "Are they getting longer or shorter? I can't decide."

"I'm only seven, you old witch. Be nice."

"Marcella *is* nice," I said. "And she isn't a witch."

"Is so!" Ruby's eyes were slits. "You take that back, Kyle, or I'll put my hex on you."

I pretended not to worry about this new word hex. But since it didn't worry me, I couldn't ask what it meant. "Then Marcella *is* a witch. But she doesn't look like one to me—she looks like anyone else."

"That's the trick," smiled Marcella. "It all has to do with the inside and the outside. You said my piano playing made you think of the sky?"

"Yeah. At night, with stars."

"Well, it only made you feel that way because I played *inside* the blues instead of outside looking in. With enough practice, anyone can play the right notes, but if I play them so they make you think of stars, then I'm inside them and I've *got* to be a witch, don't you see?"

"Maybe. I'll ask Uncle Hank."

"Suit yourself. But now we must hurry to the river while the daylight's still good."

"All right," said Ruby, "but let's not hurry *too* fast."

"Why not?" smiled Marcella. "Should we give your little legs extra time?"

"I don't need more time than anyone else," said Ruby, and for once she wasn't shouting, she barely whispered. "You're the one who has a bad heart—you should let it have a rest."

"Darling, you're quite right." Marcella leaned down to give Ruby a kiss on the top of her head. "We'll sit on this bus bench and give my ticker a rest. Very thoughtful of you."

We sat on the bench and chattered about jaywalking and jaybirds and all sorts of things—but what I *thought* about, as we chattered, was that Marcella needed to rest much more often now than when I had first met her. When we got back on our feet, she walked more slowly than she had before, and so did I, and Ruby trotted more slowly beside us. The sun was about to go down behind New Jersey, but we still had some time. When we were uptown nearly to Canal Street, we crossed the West Side Highway and made our way onto a wooden pier jutting into the river. Here and there the planks had rotted away, leaving holes that reminded me of Marcella's missing tooth. We stepped very carefully across to the far edge of the pier.

"A perfect day for our search," said Marcella. "Not a breath of wind. See how calm the water is, Kyle?"

"Yes." For once Ruby didn't break in with an opinion, which gave me some hope that she didn't understand either. "The river's calm. And so?"

"So this peaceful river is going to help you decide what your costume should be. Just lean over the edge here. Don't worry, I'll hold your hand. What do you see?"

"Nothing but water."

"We know *that,*" said Ruby. She talked tough—but didn't come close to the edge. "Do you see an octopus?"

"Nope. And no eels." I wondered what an eel might be. "Nothing but water."

"No clouds?" asked Marcella.

"Sure, but they aren't really down there. I mean, clouds are in the *sky.*"

"It looks like they're in the river to me," said Marcella.

"Me too," Ruby agreed.

"Okay, there are clouds in the river. But not real clouds."

"That's a start," said Marcella. "And what do you see closer in here, almost under the dock?"

"A face." When I smiled, the face smiled with me. "But it isn't a real face—"

"Oh? And how do you know that?"

"All right, Marcella, it's a boy who looks a lot like me."

"Excellent. And you may not know what *you* want to be for Halloween, but *that* boy does, because he lives in the river, where it's much easier to know all sorts of things. In the river—"

"Then it's simple!" I cried. "What he wants most of all is to be an explorer." The boy in the river grinned up at me. "He wants to ride on a three-humped camel across the desert."

"Which desert?" Ruby peered over the edge to see this boy explorer, and saw him, and saw a girl explorer beside him. "The desert of Morocco, right, Kyle?"

"Right. Where your skin is burned black by the sun, and you wear sandals to keep off the poison ivy—"

Marcella led us away from the edge of the pier. "And they wear white robes and turbans, to protect themselves from the sun."

I stared up at her and knew without any doubt that she was a witch, because there was the outside and there was the inside, and she knew the way inside me even better than I did.

7
The Longest Teeth

On Halloween Mom brought me over from Brooklyn and helped stitch together the costumes for Ruby and me. From her handbag she pulled a tube of makeup glue and some scraps of fake hair, so she could stick a gray fuzzy triangle onto my chin.

"Don't you want a beard?" I asked Ruby. "You'll look more like an explorer—"

"Girls don't have beards, stupid, even in Morocco. I can be a girl and still explore the desert."

"Yeah, but you'll have to cover your face, all but your eyes. Uncle Hank says the girls in Morocco hide their faces from everyone but their husbands—and I'm not your husband."

"I don't *need* a husband, and I'll go exploring without a beard or anything hiding my face." Ruby glared from the top of her baggy red robe.

"Okay, okay. But if you don't have a beard, you can't have a turban."

"Can so! Can't I, Lydia?"

"Kyle's only teasing. Boys like to tease when they talk about being husbands. If you want a turban, you can have one."

"And," I groaned, "I suppose it'll be red?"

"What do you expect? There *is* only red."

Finally we set off, cardboard daggers in hand, me in my white robe and Ruby in red. When we stopped to admire ourselves at the first big window, Ruby told Mom and Lydia to walk farther behind, since explorers don't bring their mothers to the desert. Then we rang doorbells all around her neighborhood, and scared lots of people and collected candy.

We got nice compliments for our outfits, but nothing really creepy happened until we got back to Ruby's house.

In the hallway none of the lights worked, which was strange enough. But then a shaky kind of music drifted down from the darkness—low, moaning music from somewhere above the bookshelves. The sound made me reach for my mom. But in the darkness I found only Ruby, who grabbed my hand so hard it hurt.

And then for a second it wasn't dark. Marcella's

door creaked open and the light of a candle wavered, then flickered, then went out, giving us a glimpse of a ghost hovering at the end of the hall. Ruby screamed and I screamed just as Lydia turned on the same ceiling light that hadn't worked a moment before.

"Well!" said Mom, as if nothing had happened. *"You* two were in a rush to get inside. Let's see what treats you collected."

"There was a ghost—" Ruby motioned weakly. "There, at the end of the shelves. A ghost, a candle, and—*noises."*

"Certainly," said Lydia. "It's Halloween. Are you trying to scare me, Ruby?"

"It was *there.* Kyle saw it too."

"She's telling the truth," I said. "Didn't you hear us scream?"

"How could we?" Mom smiled that play smile she puts on when she doesn't quite believe me. "We were outside when you two ran in and let the door slam in our faces. So you heard noises. And you saw—what? A curtain blowing in the breeze?"

"It was a *ghost!"* cried Ruby the red explorer, dagger held high. "Why do grown-ups always team up on kids when we're telling the truth? Marcella will believe us. Where is she?"

"Here, Miss Trumpet." Marcella stepped slowly down the stairs, a pan balanced on one hand. "I heard a whistling sound up above and thought you rascals were playing tricks. But it was only Grandmother's ghost leaving us this cake. Seems funny she would stop by when the moon isn't full. Yet it *is* Halloween, and ghosts get restless, too. Here, everyone, have a piece of crumb cake."

"Crumb cake!" screeched Ophelia from her golden cage, scaring Mom. "Crumb cake! Wanta piece a crumb cake!"

We passed the pan around and each of us ate a piece, Ophelia first. Then the front door squeaked open and stayed open for a long frozen moment while Ruby stared at me and a strangled voice whimpered, "Desert rats, desert rats, may I have some crumb cake, too?" Then there was an awful silence until a man in a black mask crept through the doorway, and of course it was Uncle Hank.

We ate more cake and drank milk until Mom said it was time to drive home to Brooklyn, perhaps Uncle Hank would give us a ride.

So I collected my candy and was ready to go, even though I didn't feel like going, when Ruby amazed us all by announcing, "No, Kyle can't go, he has to stay here tonight. I'm too scared to be alone."

"I thought," Marcella smiled, "you didn't like boys."

"Hate 'em. But I hate spooky things worse."

Mom turned to me. "Would it be too terrible, Kyle? I know you hate girls as much as Ruby hates boys, but would you mind protecting her this one night?"

"Since it's Halloween," I said, "and since Ruby's only seven and I'm nine, I guess I don't mind."

"Good!" nodded Ruby. "And I have another idea. Your uncle's driving to Brooklyn and back anyway, so we should ride along to keep him company. There are lots of goblins to see on the Brooklyn Bridge—"

Uncle Hank chuckled. "Shall we give the tykes a ride, ladies?" It was difficult to tell if, behind his black mask, he was joking or not. But when Mom went out the door with him, Ruby and I followed, and we all drove across the Brooklyn Bridge together.

"No goblins." Ruby frowned at the empty walkway beside the traffic.

"Not yet." Uncle Hank glanced at us, then into his mirror. "Just one vice president, one masked cabbie, and two oily-cheeked desert rats."

We thought that would be the end of our Halloween adventure. When Mom ran inside for my pajamas and toothbrush, the idea was that Uncle Hank would drive Ruby and me back to Laight Street where we would dream of candy corn and stomachache ghosts. But on our way up Clinton Street, a gangly vampire jumped from the sidewalk and flapped his arms so hysterically to hail us that we had to stop and let him in.

"Thirsty!" he whispered, flapping the elbows of his tuxedo. He leaned toward Ruby, who perched in front on two of my phone books. "Thirsty! Need some *blood!*"

"One inch closer," Ruby hissed, "and I'll cut off your thirsty head." She raised her cardboard knife; the vampire shrank back in terror. "Where are you going, Mr. Blood? To the hospital?"

"Smart girl! Lotsa fresh *blood* in hospital!" The vampire stretched back his lips in a horrible grin, showing his yellow fangs.

"Pilot to Desert Rat." Uncle Hank looked at me through the eyeholes of his mask. "What's our destination, Navigator? Should we drop this blood-bird in the river and let him suck some fish blood?"

"Sounds good, Pilot, unless he hurries up and tells us his address." We whizzed over the bridge, our tires singing on the metal pavement.

"Must get home," said the vampire. "Must get home by—what time you got, Pilot?"

Uncle Hank turned to me.

"Hoboken Time," I calculated, "is eleven minutes to eleven. You have to be home by midnight, Mr. Blood?"

"That's *Cinderella,*" corrected Ruby. "Don't you know anything, Kyle? Vampires have to be home by eleven for their fresh blood. After that, it goes sour."

"Well put, Dahling!" Mr. Blood sat up straighter to admire Ruby. "You have most tasty neck, I'm sure—but I'll not bite if you have me home by eleven, as you say.

Home to Crosby and Prince streets, Transylvania. Can we make it, Pilot?"

"I sincerely hope so." Uncle Hank stroked the smooth part of his neck below his beard. "Ruby can't hold more than a couple gallons. And then—?"

"Faster!" cried Mr. Blood, as if he were riding a stagecoach and Uncle Hank should whip the horses. "Home by eleven! Blood go sour!"

From the bridge we raced north on Centre Street past Chinatown to Lafayette, then turned left for a short block on Prince, and there we were, arrived at Crosby.

"Two minutes to eleven," I reported. "Good flying, Pilot. And the fare, Mr. Blood, is six dollars and twenty-five cents." When I checked with Uncle Hank, he shrugged. "But let's say three dollars, since it's Halloween and you're thirsty."

"Here's eight." He fumbled with his wallet. "And one extra for each little desert rat. I never bite neck of cute desert rat." He paused in the doorway to flash us one last awful grin, and then vanished.

"Driving a cab," I bragged to Ruby, "is a terrific life. Here's your dollar—and here's mine for me—and here's the rest for our pilot."

"Marcella and Lydia won't believe this." Ruby shook her head. "I love having a story they don't believe until they *have* to believe it because it's true." She ran her fingers over the dollar bill, and we drove a full three blocks before she got her next idea. "Is there a light in here? I want to see if there's any blood on the back seat."

"Good thinking." Uncle Hank switched on the overhead light.

Ruby turned to look, and I turned to look, and we saw it at the same instant, lying in the middle of the seat.

"A wallet!" she cried. "Mr. Blood gave us his wallet!"

Uncle Hank pulled to a stop at the edge of Broadway, reached back for the fat leather wallet, and held it in front of us. "What," he asked, the mask making his expression hard to see, "should we do with this?"

"We should look inside it," said Ruby. "Maybe it's a magic Halloween wallet that will make us rich."

Uncle Hank pulled the wallet open, and there, in a thick wad, was more money than I had ever seen. Even my uncle whistled.

"All twenties. Five hundred and forty dollars."

"It *is* magic! And we *are* rich!"

When Uncle Hank looked at her, the night grew very quiet, with only a swishing of tires as the other cabs rolled past. "Yes, we're rich if we wish to be. But I wonder if there's anything else in here. Care to look, Ruby?"

"I'd love to!" Laughing, she opened a side pocket. "No more money. Only these credit cards and a few pieces of paper. Nothing any good."

Uncle Hank spoke carefully. "Do you think Mr. Blood will miss his credit cards?"

"If he's like Lydia, he will. Last summer she lost her Macy's card and went nuts. But she called the store and they gave her a new one, so Mr. Blood can do the same thing. Let's throw out the credit cards and divide the money. Right, Kyle?"

"I don't know. What should we do, Uncle?"

"You mean with the credit cards?" Something in his voice told me he was saying more than he was saying.

"I mean with everything. Could you take off that mask, Uncle, so you don't look so weird?"

"Sure." He slipped the mask off and rubbed his nose. "I must have looked like a thief with that thing on."

"No, just weird. What should we do with all the money, Uncle?"

"You tell *me,*" he said. Which wasn't anything like what my dad would have said.

"Well, *Dad* would say we have to give it back."

"I'm sure he would," said Uncle Hank. A truck rumbled past, making us shake in its wind. "But he isn't here, and he'll never know about this unless we tell him."

"Right!" agreed Ruby. "And Lydia won't know, or Marcella—"

"That's true." Uncle Hank's voice was very soft. I was glad his mask was off, so I could see that his eyes were friendly. "But Ruby, *why* won't we tell Lydia or Marcella about the money?"

"Because they'd get mad and say we were stealing and—" Realizing what she had said, she clapped a hand over her mouth.

His voice grew even softer. "And—would we be stealing?"

Ruby beat one tiny fist on Uncle Hank's knee, making him wince. "No! It's not stealing because Mr. Blood *gave* us the money. Right?"

Uncle Hank rubbed his knee. "Is that right, Kyle? Did Mr. Blood—"

"No. He was in such a hurry, he dropped the wallet on his way out."

"And so? If he didn't give us the money—"

"Then we're taking it. Stealing it."

"But no one will know!" pouted Ruby.

"Uncle Hank will know."

"He won't *tell* anyone!"

"Still, he'll know. He'll know that we're robbers. And robbing people is wrong."

Ruby groaned with disgust.

"That's what it comes down to," said Uncle Hank. "Tell me this, Ruby. If someone robbed *you,* would it be wrong?"

She nodded once, furiously.

"—Then isn't it wrong if *you* rob someone *else?*"

Ruby was thinking hard. "But even if we wanted to

give back the money, we don't know where Mr. Blood lives."

"Ah, but we do. Right on this driver's license it gives Mr. Blood's address, even though his name here is Kronski, not Blood. He lives where we dropped him off, at 108 Crosby Street. What time do you have, Navigator?"

"Twenty minutes—twenty after eleven."

"Do we *have* to take it back?" wailed Ruby.

"I know it's a rough choice, but yes, we do." Uncle Hank pulled the cab into the traffic of Broadway, made a left on Canal and another left up Centre Street. "Look there," he pointed. "See those gorillas lumbering down the sidewalk?"

"Don't *want* to." Ruby scowled at her dagger but then peeked to the side as we passed.

"Scary-looking brutes, aren't they?"

"Are *not.* I hate you."

"Yes, I know," said Uncle Hank. "But don't hate me too much until we see what happens at Mr. Blood's house."

First Ruby claimed she didn't want to go inside. But when Uncle Hank said she could carry the wallet and do the talking, the temptation was too great. At the front door he lifted her up so she could shout into the voice box.

"Hey, Mr. Blood? This is Ruby the Desert Rat, from the yellow taxi, and I have a surprise for you—"

"Praise Allah!" cried a tinny voice from the speaker. "How worried I've been—Dahling, I love you, I *love* you, come straight up to 4B, I'll make some juice." The front door buzzed and in we went.

A man opened the door to 4B, a tall thin man dressed in slippers and a blue robe. He had gray hair and looked nothing like a vampire, and he carried an apparently normal tray loaded with four glasses and a clear high pitcher filled with—filled with—

"A brand new flavor of Kool-Aid." He led us into a room that held not even one coffin. "Quite an odd taste, but ideal for Halloween." He seated us around a low table and poured our glasses full.

"Kool-Aid?" Ruby squinched her eyes into their most stubborn frown.

"Yes, Dahling. Such a lovely shade of red, don't you think? So rich, so flavorful—and *healthy*? The best thing for you!"

"Sure," she said, "Dahling." For once Ruby didn't seem too crazy about red. "Why do you dress so funny, anyhow? Are you some TV guy?"

"No," explained Mr. Kronski. "For a living I make rings. Magical rings, you might say, of silver. Drink your Kool-Aid and I'll show you some of my work."

Ruby waited until Mr. Kronski drank, and so did I,

but still we wouldn't take a sip. We studied Uncle Hank as he swallowed a huge gulp and made a strange face, then licked his lips.

"Delicious!" he grinned. "Salty, but pretty good. What's wrong with you two? Scared?"

"Never." Ruby closed her eyes and took a baby sip. Then a bigger sip. "Ah. It's all right, Kyle, you can drink now."

I did, but cautiously. The juice was much darker red than any Kool-Aid I had ever tried, and it had a weird flavor, but I drank every drop and felt only a little like throwing up.

Ruby reached inside her desert robe. "Here's your present, dahling Kronski. I wanted to keep it but Kyle said that would be stealing, he said *Hank* would know even if Lydia didn't. So here it is."

"Thank you ever so much." Mr. Kronski slipped the wallet into a pocket of his robe without even checking to see that all his money was inside. From the same pocket he took two rings, one small and one smaller, which he handed to me and Ruby.

"For us to *keep?*" Her eyes gleamed. "And they're really silver?"

"The very finest—dug up by the Indians of Mexico." He led us to the door. "Do your rings fit, my little desert rats?"

"Perfectly," I said.

"Perfectly," said Ruby.

"I thought they would. And here, please take something else for your trouble." He pulled the wallet from his silk pocket, opened it, and handed each of us—Uncle Hank, Ruby, and me—a twenty-dollar bill. "You've made this a memorable Halloween." When he smiled, his teeth showed, but they didn't look longer or sharper than the teeth of anyone else.

We thanked him and thanked him again, and Ruby called him Dahling one last time, and we took the elevator to the street floor. Outside, the sky was crowded with stars that gazed down on us with great admiration.

We climbed into the cab and headed south toward Laight Street.

"Lydia," said Ruby, "will never believe this."

8
The Woman in the Moon

Since Dad was drinking worse than ever, Mom decided it was best for me to spend my weekends at Ruby's house for a while. So, on a hot Friday in November, Uncle Hank drove me across to Manhattan.

"Uncle, why does Mom call our house the War Zone?"

"Why do you think? What *is* a war zone, anyway?"

"On TV, it's where people get killed."

He steered us through the angry traffic across from City Hall. "You're right, people can get killed in a war zone. But other things can also get killed. Things such as love—"

"And my dad is killing it? Like the Rich Man, when he threw Lydia off the tower? *That* was a war zone."

"Yes, it was." Uncle Hank didn't honk even when all

the cabs around us honked. "But she lived through it, didn't she?"

"Dad wouldn't throw Mom off a castle."

"No. Old George wouldn't do that."

"But he did throw a jar against the kitchen wall. A jar of low-cal mayonnaise."

"Yeah." Uncle Hank waited for the green arrow to let us make our left onto Chambers. "He told me about that. Your dad's an unhappy man, Kyle. He's doing things even *he* can't believe. In a war zone, we all do things we can't understand. You know what I mean?"

"Not really." It was November but hotter than August. We had our windows open, and I didn't understand why it was so hot when the trees were bare and ready for winter. "No, Uncle. What *do* you mean?"

"Well, look. Have you ever had a friend who was very special, but you did something cruel to this friend anyway? Because you couldn't be kind like you wanted to be?"

"I don't think so, Uncle."

"Well *I* did, when I was exactly your age. I was nine, and there was a ten-year-old girl living next door, and I was wild about her but couldn't say so. I couldn't be gentle the way I wanted to be. So instead I was mean. One day I saw her standing beside a garbage can, and her shoulder was so pretty I wanted to touch it, just once, to see if it felt as smooth as it looked."

"Her *shoulder,* Uncle?" I had to laugh. "By a *garbage* can? You're making this up."

"Kyle, I can still see the curve of her shoulder—it was a hot day like this, and she wore a sleeveless blouse. But instead of touching her softly, as I wanted to, I ran over and gave her a shove against the garbage can—all of a sudden, not even aware what I was doing."

"So she thought you hated her."

"Probably." Uncle Hank looked across at City Hall. "What else *could* she think? When actually I liked her too much to keep control of my feelings. So I hurt her instead of being nice."

"And that's what Mom and Dad are doing now? In the War Zone?"

"It's hard to know. But people don't always mean what they do or say. If your folks aren't being kind to each other, it doesn't mean they wouldn't rather be kind, deeper down. You see?"

"I don't like thinking about the War Zone. I wish it would snow. Dad likes the snow because it's cool and quiet and every flake has six sides. Maybe he'll be kinder when it snows. Maybe at Christmas."

"Yeah," said Uncle Hank. "Maybe." The light on Broadway changed from red to green; a cop waved circles with his white glove; we inched ahead. Drivers all around us honked and honked, but not my uncle. He frowned into the distance and didn't seem concerned with the traffic at all.

* * *

We picked up Ruby and Marcella and drove to Central Park for some roller-skating. Lydia stayed home because she was in the middle of painting a picture, and said she painted best when she was alone. But I suspected she limped when she roller-skated, and didn't want Uncle Hank to see.

We shouted good-bye to her and drove up the West Side Highway, along the Hudson River blazing under the sun. The river was so cheerful I forgot about Lydia's fall from the castle and about the War Zone in Brooklyn. We drove to the park and rented skates and laced them on.

Ruby was small even for a seven-year-old, but she was quick, and had skated often with Marcella, while I'd only gone once. So she had an easier time staying on her feet, and moved faster, even with short legs. She wore a cute red skirt and a red top, and, although I didn't say so, in her red elbow pads and kneepads she looked pretty flashy. Beside her I felt clumsy, but I was too proud to take Marcella's hand. If Ruby could skate on her own, so could I.

She pointed and laughed at me and skated red circles around me, and rushed over and knocked me off balance, tripping me onto the pavement. Then, laughing her nastiest laugh, she zipped away. For a minute Uncle Hank and Marcella said nothing. Then Uncle pulled me to my feet.

"You aren't hurt, are you, Navigator? Did your padding protect you?"

"Sure." I pretended to be like the tough football guys who were such heroes for my dad. "Only hit my kneepad. But why did she do that?"

"Because she didn't dare hold your hand, I suppose, and had to do something cruel instead. Like I did to that ten-year-old girl beside the garbage can."

"Uncle, you're not making sense."

He shrugged. "It's like your folks in Brooklyn. Adults can be mean, kids can be mean—"

"Well if Ruby wants to be mean, I can be mean right back."

"Don't be *too* mean. Remember, she's your friend most of the time. She asked you to stay at her house—"

"Huh! Because she was scared of ghosts? I can be mean if she can."

Ruby came skating back, still laughing her sharp laugh. She was going to pass close beside me, but I dodged into her way and forced her off the path—and on the grass her skates didn't do any good. She had to run as if she had on thick clumpy boots, and I ran clump-clump after her, laughing my own laugh now because if it was slow for me to run on roller skates, it was slower for Ruby, with her tiny red-skirted legs.

Then I did like in football, flinging my arms around her legs and dragging her to the ground—and suddenly, before I knew it myself, I did something I'd never seen any football player do. Ruby's leg was in front of my face, and without thinking I kissed it, fast and hard, on the smooth rosy part just below her kneepad. And she was so mad I had tackled her, and was screaming so loud, she had no idea I kissed her. A kiss was way worse than a tackle, and would have made her ten times madder, but it was over in an instant and she never knew it had happened.

But Uncle Hank knew, and Marcella. They stood on the path, in the breezy sunshine, shaking with laughter.

"I tackled her, Uncle."

"You certainly did. Welcome to the War Zone."

"Let me up!" howled Ruby. "You bully, let me up!"

I let her up, and she streaked down the path while Marcella and I sat on a bench, catching our breath. Uncle Hank skated slowly after Ruby.

"You promise not to tell her about that little—that little kiss?"

"I promise." Marcella chuckled, making a great whistle between her front teeth. "Kyle, what a stitch you gave me. Strained my ticker worse than roller-skating." She patted her purple chest as if to tame something inside it.

"What's your ticker, Marcella?"

"Oh, that's my heart, my engine, the thing that makes me go. When it stops, I stop."

"When it stops, you *die?*"

"Then I die." She pulled me close. "Don't be alarmed, Kyle, it can't be as tragic as all that."

"But I don't want you to die. I promise not to make you laugh, if it's bad for your heart."

"Nonsense!" She pulled me closer. "It's *good* for my heart to laugh, and to see you loving and hating that red devil. My heart's had its full share of fun, believe me. It doesn't feel cheated."

"But I don't want you to die." I had never heard anyone talk about death so cheerfully. "Will you die—soon, Marcella?"

"Probably. But I've said that for years, ever since my boyfriend gave me these skates and promptly keeled over himself—and I was scarcely sixty then. We have large hearts in my family, much larger than normal—but not pieced together quite right, which means they run rougher and wear out quicker than the standard model."

"But you're *old,* Marcella! You've lasted a long time!"

"That's what I'm saying. I've been very lucky, I've had long and good use of this ticker. But sometimes after I laugh so hard or skate up such a steep hill as this one, I give it a rest. Lately, I've just had to rest it more often. Shall we roll? I feel fine again."

She balanced me beside her, and we coasted down the long lazy hill, with Marcella's hair floating out behind us like a silky white banner. At the bottom, beside Uncle Hank, Ruby stood with her hands on her hips, laughing at our slowness. I was glad to see her, and was glad her laughing finally seemed friendly.

"Tonight," Ruby whispered, after supper and dish-washing, and after Lydia's story of two squirrels named Jill and Jeb, blue and pink, who lived in a clock and had skis for feet—"Tonight I'll show you my roof. I meant to show you on Halloween, but then we met Mr. Blood and I forgot. Anyway, tonight's better. The moon should be full tonight, Marcella says—and she says you can't see the moon so well from *any* place as from my roof." Her eyes narrowed and grew blacker, and I knew that somewhere behind them, an idea was hatching. "And today was hot, so tonight will be warm, so we can *sleep* on the roof! Under the full moon! Marcella says sleeping under a full moon does wonders, it makes *you* shine, too. I'll go ask if we can sleep there—"

"Okay," I said—but my mind was on something else. "Is Marcella going to die?"

Ruby tilted her head to one side, like Ophelia. "Lydia says that maybe—*maybe* she will. *Maybe.* And it might happen soon, Lydia says—so I should be ready."

"How can you be ready for—that?"

"I'm not sure. But I *think* Lydia said the way to be ready is to *not pretend.*"

"Not pretend what?"

"Not pretend it won't happen."

I thought this over. "But I *want* to pretend. I don't want Marcella to die."

Just as I said this, Marcella entered the room, a sleeping bag under her arm. "I heard you talking from out in the hallway. Eavesdropping is impolite, but witches can't help themselves, and I had to catch every word. You have the perfect idea, Ruby. You can show Kyle the roof, and we can lie in our bedrolls and enjoy the moon—and I'll tell you about death, if you wish, and then we can sleep. Some peaceful death-chatter is always the best lullaby."

Before going to the roof we told Lydia our plan, so she wouldn't worry when she found our beds empty. We didn't have to tell Uncle Hank; this was a Friday night and he was out cruising the streets, raking in big tips to go with big fares from the big-spending weekend crowd.

Ruby led us up the last flight of stairs and opened the trap door up into the night. "My roof," she said, holding the door open. "The best roof in New York."

I could see why she thought so: the place we climbed into didn't seem like a roof so much as a misty garden. And not a backyard garden, like ours in Brooklyn, squashed between one brownstone and the next. No, this was a garden in the sky. Even though I knew it couldn't be really, it seemed to be floating. And like gray and black clouds, shadows stretched down to us from the higher buildings all around.

"Do you like the vines?" Ruby asked. "They look gray at night, but in the daytime, since autumn came, they've been the best shade of red. And in the summer we have lots of different ferns, and Lydia's palm trees from her studio, and all sorts of wildflowers—there, along that wall. In the summer it's a *jungle,* Kyle, with everything but snakes. On nights with no moon, we light candles and tell scary stories. But tonight we won't need candles."

"Where *is* the moon?" I asked. "Over there?"

"Yeah, behind that building. When's it coming out, Marcella?"

"Soon, Miss Ruby." In the tall building just across Laight Street, a single light went on in a single window, and just as suddenly went out. The bright blink of light made the building look twice as dark as before, and twice as high. "Let's make up our beds now, so when the moon comes out we can study it comfortably."

Ruby and I ran downstairs to get the bedding and to give Marcella's ticker a rest. It took us three trips to carry up the folding cots and pillows and sleeping bags, but soon we had everything arranged, and we burrowed into our beds and admired the view. On the black buildings around us perched round little water tanks, with roofs like tiny pointed hats that shone white where the moonlight hit them.

Marcella lay between Ruby and me. "The moon won't be long now. See where its first glow is creeping over that roof? But while we wait, we can listen to the river. It's so close I hear it whispering."

"Is the river whispering," I asked, "about death?"

"Yes, child. It says that life is the same as a river, and we're all a part of it, because when old-timers like me reach the end of life, young snips like you are high in the mountains, splashing into brooks that will grow into wider brooks when you're twelve years old, and streams when you're twenty, and then a wider and wider river, flowing always more slowly, more peacefully, until you, like me, reach the ocean many years later. But it won't be sad, since you'll know that up in the hills the little brooks are splashing and laughing. And so it never ends, the river, it flows and it flows."

"But Marcella," I asked, "what happens when you get to New York City and the ocean? Do you disappear forever? Or do you go to—heaven?"

She reached across to touch my cheek. I could tell, even in the dim light before the moon appeared, that she was smiling her smile with its tooth gone. "Heaven sounds pretty dull to me. Sitting in the fog, strumming on some harp day after day, with no blues piano, no trombone? But it won't be dull to flow out into the ocean. So many faraway creatures to see! So many places! And such eavesdropping, Kyle, under the open windows of all those ships! Such adventures!"

"But when you're dead, you don't see anything.

When you're dead you're just gone. That's what my dad says. Everything's over, finished."

"Maybe so. But I've had so much sunshine that gliding into an ocean of darkness doesn't worry me. It sounds restful. Look now, the moon's peeping out, her face is showing—"

"*Her* face?"

"Yes, Kyle. That's my grandmother up there. She'll watch until we're asleep—I think Ruby's asleep already—and then she'll drift down and set a fresh pan of crumb cake in Lydia's cupboard. You'll see in the morning."

"And when you die, will she still bring the crumb cake every full moon, or will she stop?"

"Don't worry, she won't stop. It's quite possible I'll help with her baking."

The light of the moon was so strong on us now, I didn't have to guess that Marcella was smiling—I could see her face beaming up toward the moon and could see her long hair fanned out silver across the pillow. She smiled, and the woman in the moon smiled, and when I fell asleep that November night, among the silver vines of that jungle roof, I must have got something confused, because I dreamed Marcella's face floated up and up until she was that same kindly woman beaming down from the moon.

9

Home to the North Pole

When the weather turned cold and the first snow came, my dad didn't smile at the change, as he had the year before. He didn't smile at anything now, not even the idea of Christmas. From the front window he stared out at the dancing flakes and grumbled that snow made the sidewalks slippery. Then he poured himself another drink and turned up the volume on the TV.

That was when Mom said the TV drove her crazy and turned it off and glared down at him in his chair. The room was very quiet, but not for long. Soon it was filled with the same old sounds: first angry whispers, then nasty words, then nastier shouts, and finally the worst noise of all, when his hand hit her face and she stumbled to the floor. I shut my eyes and tried pretending it wasn't real. But my ears couldn't shut, and they heard everything.

When Mom got up, she didn't say a word, didn't even cry. She held one hand to her cheek and walked to their bedroom and packed a suitcase. She didn't cry even when her eye swelled shut under its red bruise. When we went out the door I said good-bye to Dad, but he must not have heard me because he didn't say anything back.

Our cab was halfway across the bridge before Mom stopped shaking. She pounded one knee with her hand, then turned to look at me. "Honey," she said, staring at me with her one good eye, "where can we *go?*"

"We can go to your friend Susan's, Mom, like we tried doing that other time."

"Yes." She rubbed her puffy cheek as if to help it feel better. "We could go there. But Susan has a small place, only a big room, really—hardly big enough for even *one* visitor."

"—And there are two of us."

"Yes," Mom whispered. "Two of us." She started crying, silently, with one arm around me. There was nothing I could say to help, but I tried anyway.

"I could go stay at Ruby's, Mom."

"Without *me?*"

"Sure—then there would just be one of you at your friend Susan's."

"But I'm your *mother,* Honey—you're my little *boy.*"

"Not so little," I said, even if I had felt like a baby when I'd heard Dad hit her.

"Are you *sure,* Kyle? You wouldn't mind too terribly if I let you stay at Ruby's for a while?"

"I wouldn't mind. I like staying there, and going to a new school might be kind of fun."

She smiled so painfully that I wondered if her puffy eye was starting to hurt. "Later on, we can talk about schools. For now we just have to make it through tomorrow. You're *sure* you don't mind staying alone?"

"I won't be alone, I'll have Ruby and Lydia and Marcella—and Ophelia the talking bird, and even Uncle Hank, when he visits Lydia."

"Oh?" said Mom. "I suppose he visits often."

I tried cheering her up by poking a little fun at Uncle. "He's *courting* Lydia, he says. And he likes their house because they don't have TV."

"That sounds like Hank. But don't *you* miss TV?"

"At their house, I don't really need one."

"You feel at home with them."

"Yeah, I guess so. It's a friendly place."

Mom looked so sad I knew I'd said the wrong thing. "You're more at home in Ruby's house, aren't you?"

"Kind of. They don't fight like you and—" I stopped myself, because Mom was gazing out at the cables of the bridge now, and when she cried, the tears made her wince when they dripped from her swollen eye. So I didn't say any more, didn't tell her I knew it was my fault, and I knew their fighting wouldn't have started if I hadn't been born.

We drove through the snow to Ruby's house.

It was all so strange.

The very next weekend, when he saw that Mom and I weren't coming back, Dad started paying more attention to me. On the first Saturday in December, he picked me up at Ruby's house and we took a cab to Madison Square Garden and saw the Knicks play Detroit. The game was fun, except he talked so much about Mom and how she didn't understand him that the game wasn't much fun after all.

The next day *she* took me out, to a movie and then a fancy supper, and at the restaurant she kept talking about *him,* and how he never listened to her side of an argument—which wasn't much fun either.

During the week they left me alone, and I had a good time with Ruby, and went riding with Uncle Hank, and I never missed TV at all. But then the next weekend brought the same thing again, Dad on Saturday, Mom on Sunday, each complaining about the other when they weren't asking me what toys I wanted for Christmas. Mostly what I wanted was to ride to new places with Uncle Hank, but I couldn't tell them that.

But I could tell him.

"Yeah," he agreed. "This *is* fun, isn't it? Looking at

Christmas lights, and store windows, and people scooting along as if someone would spank them if they slowed down. We even see Santa Claus now and then."

"All the time," I said, but without pleasure. I wasn't in much of a mood for Santa Claus. "There are Santas everywhere."

"Are there?" Uncle Hank tried to look what Mom would have called flabbergasted, but I knew he was kidding. "I thought there was only one Santa, and he moved around, never staying in any spot more than a minute—"

"Don't be silly, Uncle, we just passed one by the cathedral, and now there's another, ringing his bell."

"Well so there is. What do you know." He pulled over at the corner of Fifth and Forty-fourth, where a Santa stood shaking his gold bell. "Hey, old man!" Uncle leaned across and rolled my window down. "Hey! Old man!"

First Santa scowled, but then he saw me and smiled. "May I help you, gentlemen?"

"Yeah," barked Uncle Hank, like the rudest cabbie in New York. "What's your name, anyway?"

"That's a peculiar thing to be asking a fat man dressed in red, on the seventeenth of December. You don't recognize me without my reindeer?" Santa puffed grandly on his pipe.

"Maybe I do," said Uncle Hank, "and maybe not. You don't ring a bell too badly, and your beard looks real—but we need to be sure. So tell us, where do you live?"

"The North Pole, obviously! Everyone knows that!"

"Let's say I believe you. Then tell me this—what's the cab fare run you to the North Pole? Unless maybe you take the subway home—"

"Are you joking? I ride behind my deer, except when Rudolph has a sniffle, like today. Yes, tonight I'll take a cab home. Thirteen or fourteen bucks to the North Pole. Up the river, you know—"

"And when does your shift end?"

"Eight o'clock. Still an hour to go, and it's been a long day out here busting my chops. Ding-ding-ding, ho-ho-ho—"

"Then Nephew Kyle and I will be back at eight on the button. We'll treat you to a free ride, since it's Christmas. Free, that is, if you're nice to the kids."

"I see only one kid."

"There'll be one more," I explained. "A pipsqueak named Ruby, who's seven and wears nothing but red."

"I like her already. Good. I'll be waiting."

"Right." Uncle Hank pulled us away from the curb.

I looked behind us to where Santa stood ringing his golden bell as he rocked backward and forward and smiled up into the snowflakes.

Uncle Hank nudged me. "What's the time, Navigator?"

"Hoboken Time is seven o'clock and six minutes."

"Perfect. That gives this North Pole Express fifty-four minutes to fetch Miss Ruby. Say, you're right, there's another Santa, and another! What a puzzle. Do you think ours is a fake?"

"Uncle, I think we should try him out on Ruby. She thinks she knows everything—"

"Good thinking, Kid. We'll go get her and see."

But Ruby told Uncle Hank she'd rather stay home and paint than go exploring with us. Across from Ophelia the talking bird, she sat near Marcella, and tried looking important, and smeared blobs of red paint onto a black cardboard box.

"It's snowing out," said Marcella, from her armchair by the window. "Coming down dizzier by the minute. If I were feeling stronger, *I* would certainly go inspect this Santa fellow. But I need to stay here and rest."

"I won't go," said Ruby, "if you won't."

"But the taxi crew will take fine care of you," replied Marcella. "And I'll be right here when you get back."

"You promise?"

"Yes, Sweetie."

"You won't be dead?"

"No, Ruby. I promise."

"You won't faint like you did last week when you went skating without me?"

"I didn't *faint,* Ruby. As I told you later, I felt a little more tired than usual, and sat down for a longer rest than usual."

Marcella smiled when she said this, but we all knew the truth was more serious. She hadn't gone skating once since her scare in the park, and she felt so tired now that she hardly ever left the house. Climbing stairs was so much work for her now that when she wanted to visit the roof, Uncle Hank had to carry her. Ruby and I spent a lot of our free time sitting with her, listening to records together and painting pictures.

"Just think," Uncle Hank told Ruby. "Maybe we'll get lost in a blizzard on our way to the North Pole. Then we'll end up in China, or in Switzerland, where the mountains are filled with dogs that have brandy barrels slung from their collars."

"You're making fun of me." But Ruby couldn't help smiling; she loved the way Uncle made fun of her.

"All right, I'll show you." He brought out Marcella's globe and pointed to where China lay, off west of New Jersey, and Switzerland, far east of Queens—and Santa's own North Pole, spinning above everything.

"*That's* where we're going?" Ruby shook her red parka down from its hook. "Why didn't you tell me? Should I wear my boots?"

"Good idea. Then if a nasty elf kicks you, you can kick back."

She wiggled her red-socked feet into her boots. We kissed Marcella good-bye, took three extra phone books for Ruby to sit on, and drove north through the snow to midtown.

Our Santa, the fattest on Fifth Avenue, was as polite as he was plump. "May I sit in the front, please? I get so nervous when I don't have my reindeer to drive—I need to see the road."

"Sure," I answered. "I can sit in back."

"That won't be necessary. At least not if Miss Scarlet will sit on my lap. Ruby, is it?" Lightly picking her up, Santa wedged himself inside and propped her on one of his knees.

"They *told* you my name."

Santa raised his white eyebrows and admitted nothing. "Such a delightful coat, Ruby. I love your color scheme."

"Yours isn't bad either." She settled back a bit in his arms. We rolled across town, our wheels muffled by the shifting snow. "But you don't really live at the North Pole—?"

"Indeed I do. Say, what's this I'm sitting on? Ah! The Bronx directory! And here's Brooklyn! What a multitude I'm squashing with all my pounds!" He laid the phone books on the back seat beside his bulging brown sack. "Do you always sit on so many millions of people, Ruby, when you drive around town?"

"Always. So I can see out, you know, because I'm kind of small, like your—your—"

"My elves. Yes, they are tiny mites, much tinier than you and not nearly so pretty. But they do fine work. All except Flugel, who's been a bit off, lately."

"Who's he?" Ruby's suspicion was fading.

"One of my tiny guys—specializes in musical toys. Horns, mostly." Santa licked at a white ragged tip of his mustache. "Little Flugel. He misses Bavaria."

"Where's Barbaria?" Her suspicion was gone. "Near China?"

Uncle Hank chuckled. "No, Ruby, it's near that place Switzerland I told you about. You know—"

"Sure," she sighed. "With the mountains and brandy-barrel dogs."

This gave Santa a good ho-ho-ho, bobbing Ruby on his lap like a boat in a bathtub. "Your geography is excellent. But would you mind too terribly if I lit my old pipe? Carved by Fritz, who comes from Switzerland, funny enough. Troublesome imp—never in at bedtime—but no one can match him at pipe whittling. May I?"

"Go right ahead. Marcella used to smoke a pipe, but she stopped because of her ticker. Did Fripp carve her pipe, too?"

"I expect so, if it was any good. And exactly who is Marcella?"

"Just an old witch I know. She wears purple and plays piano. You'd like her."

"I'm sure I would." With one finger, Santa tapped

tobacco into his pipe. "I like most people, but some I like particularly. Including everyone in this taxi, even its rather gruff driver."

"Even—me?" I asked.

"Naturally you." Santa sucked a flame into his pipe. He puffed once, twice, filling the cab with a rich blue sweetness—and all through this puffing, his eyes never left mine. "Why *not* you? Is there some good reason I shouldn't like you?"

"You know who's been naughty. And you know who's been nice."

"True." Santa nodded like a grandfather from the sea or the mountains or the North Pole. "But, Kyle, I find it hard to believe you could have been naughty. Not in any way that really matters—"

"This really matters." I looked out at the flakes twisting down from the night sky. Traffic poked toward the West Side Highway; at the end of the block, a cop sat high on a gleaming black horse. "My parents are getting divorced." I concentrated on studying the cop. "And it's my fault."

"Your fault?" Santa repeated. "I wonder."

"My dad even said he's tired of me."

"I see. And you don't have any brothers or sisters," said Santa, understanding completely. He pulled off his red stocking cap and used its fringe to polish his glasses. With his wavy gray hair hanging loose, and his eyes no longer hidden, he looked very tired and very wise. "You're all alone, so it's your fault, and no one else's fault, that your parents are miserable. Is that how you've been naughty, Kyle?"

"If I was never born," I whispered, watching the cop on his horse, "they'd be happy now. They'd have lots of money and Dad would be a partner and he wouldn't drink so much and he wouldn't hit Mom."

"If you hadn't been born," Santa repeated. "That's a very big if."

Uncle Hank gave me the saddest look I'd ever seen him give anyone. Ruby's eyes were wide and black, and for once she didn't say a word. The traffic had stopped. No one honked, maybe because the snow was so peaceful, or because the horseback cop looked so strong with his blue cape and his shoulders covered in snow. A walkie-talkie crackled from its holster on his belt, but he didn't answer it; he sat straight on his horse and looked ever so handsome.

Santa rolled down the side window and took in a breath of snowy air. "It's surprising you should say such a thing, Kyle. I mean, about the divorce being your fault. You see, I have helpers all over New York—in all five boroughs—who keep an eye on all the children to see who's been naughty or nice. And they told me about you."

"They did?" Our cab rolled a few feet closer to the cop on his horse.

"Yes, indeed." Santa placed his silver-rimmed glasses

back on his nose and peered through them at me. "They told me this divorce is not your fault. Not one bit. Your parents are miserable, as you say—but it's their own fault, not yours, and *they* must work it out. That's what my helpers tell me, so I stand by what I said earlier. Not only do I *like* you, Kyle, I like you especially well, because you're a very special boy, even if you do sit on phone books full of people."

He must have seen inside me then, to where I felt full of sunlight even though it was cold and dark outside, because he went softly ho-ho-ho from deep in his belly, bouncing Ruby more gently than before, and making her go ho-ho-ho too, out the open window up at the cop on his high black horse. He looked down at us where we had stopped for the light.

"Ho-ho yourself," smiled the cop. His horse pawed the street as if it wanted supper.

"We've got Santa Claus in our cab!"

"Then you're a lucky little girl." The cop moved his horse closer and waved down to Santa. "I wasn't that lucky when I was your age."

"But you've got a pretty horse," said Ruby. "And a radio on your belt—does it play Christmas music?"

"Not tonight." He pulled the walkie-talkie loose and handed it down to her. "Only talk."

Ruby held it to her ear and listened to the voices. They sounded like characters from a TV with bad reception. "Can *you* talk into it?"

"Sure I can. Here." He took back the walkie-talkie, pushed its button, and said impressively, "Hey, Spud, you read me?"

"Loud and clear, High Boots. Who've you got?"

"Just Santa Claus, sitting in a cab here with the cutest pair of kids on the West Side."

"Some guys got all the luck," crackled Spud, whoever and wherever he was.

The light turned green. We waved good-bye to High Boots, twisted up onto the West Side Highway, and rolled silently through the deepening snow.

Ruby touched Santa's silver buttons, her eyebrows drawing together as they often did when she was sprouting an idea. She turned to Uncle Hank. *"You* should get a radio like that. And then, when you drive past our house in the middle of the night, you could talk through the air and tell Lydia how much you *love* her."

"That's a thought." Uncle Hank winked at Santa, and we all went ho-ho-ho together, me loudest, because I felt gladder than I had felt in a very long time.

I felt so glad that I truly did want to stay awake until we reached the North Pole, so I could see what Fritz and Flugel looked like. But Santa's puffing was so drowsy, and the snow was so dreamy, that I leaned against Uncle Hank, and felt his arm strong around my shoulder, and I slept.

10
Fripp and Foogel

Day by day Marcella grew weaker until she never left the house—even lying down bothered her. But in the nights before Christmas she would sit on the roof, bundled in purple blankets, to watch the stars and the moon and the giant night clouds. Every night her face looked thinner, and I came to see how people believed in ghosts, since Marcella was turning into one herself. All but her eyes, which didn't lose their sparkle even in the dark.

"Do you feel the river, Kyle?" She sighed a white breath up into the night. "It's so close, the river. I can feel it moving, always moving. Do you feel it?"

"When you talk about it, I do. It's moving out to the ocean." I didn't want to think about the river.

She smiled, as if hearing my thoughts. "When I die, I won't be buried in a cemetery. Too crowded. Too much nasty gossip. This old body will be burned into ashes, and you can take them—you and Ruby—and scatter them onto the river."

"That sounds nice, Marcella." It *did* sound nice when she spoke of it so calmly, out under the night stars. And that was the miracle. I didn't want to think about Marcella dying—but when *she* talked about putting ashes in the river, it didn't feel quite so scary.

"Would you do that for me, Kyle?" She took my hand, her fingers warm and smooth around mine. "I tried telling Ruby, but she's still too young, she won't listen. You're more ready. When the time comes, she'll be ready too, she'll want to help. But I had to discuss it with you now."

"Does Lydia know about it? About—burning you?"

"She's known for years. And I've explained it to your uncle, and your mother as well—so you won't be alone in explaining it to Ruby."

"I miss my—" But I couldn't finish saying it.

"You miss your mother?"

I nodded, twice.

"Of *course* you miss her, Sweetie! But she's nearby, you can see her whenever you wish—"

"I know. And I mean, I like living here. I'd *rather* live here. And Mom comes to see me almost every day, you know—"

"Kyle, of course she does, as soon as she gets off her job—and your father visits, too."

"Yeah, when he isn't too busy."

"They haven't stopped loving you just because they fight between each other—"

"No. That's what Uncle says, too. They're going through a hard time, he says."

"—Something we adults call a period of adjustment." Marcella smiled. "Life is full of adjustments. Changes. Even death, if you look at it with some humor, is only one more adjustment."

"It is?"

"Yes, Warlock Navigator, and you'll be very helpful when the time comes to explain all this to Ruby." Marcella breathed a white cloud into the sky. "These are lovely clean nights before Christmas, feeling the river so close." She studied my eyes and saw the question there. "No, death doesn't worry me at all." She smiled so fondly, and held my hand so warmly, that it was hard to believe we had known each other just a few months. "But something else does worry me, and I have to warn you about it."

I waited.

"This divorce of your parents. And with Christmas coming—"

"Santa told me it isn't my fault."

"Yes, I heard. And of course he's right, it isn't your fault in the slightest. Still, it will make Christmas difficult for you, and you should be prepared. Even though your parents both love you, they may come out with some strange accusations, trying to hurt each other through you. But please remember one thing. Whenever they want you to take sides, but you don't *want* to take sides, and the struggle wears you out and you need new strength, you can fly back here, to this roof, in a second. To the night sky and the river flowing past. Whenever you need to feel stronger, in your mind you can return to the roof and the river, and then you'll be able to face things. Do you see what I mean?"

"And if I can do that when my parents fight, can I do it any other time, too? Like—when you die?"

"That would be a perfect time. Any time you wish is a perfect time."

"I'll remember."

And it was good she gave me her roof as a charm against pain, because Christmas Eve with my dad, and Christmas morning with my mom, had too many bright smiles and promises. He took me to the Tavern on the Green, an expensive restaurant in Central Park, and she took me to the Russian Tea Room, an even more expensive place. He gave me flashy football videos I didn't feel like watching but had to *say* I felt like watching; she gave me fancy leather boots I knew I'd ruin in the slush. With every new gift, I wished myself back to Marcella's roof and her purple soothing voice.

But that afternoon I learned that the best part of Christmas—that year at least—was not fancy presents from Mom and Dad. The best part was being together with Uncle Hank and Lydia and Ruby in the glow of Marcella's smile.

And there *were* some good surprises. Roller skates for me and Ruby—the adjustable kind that clamped onto our shoes—and a grown-up pair for Uncle Hank, all from Marcella. Lydia had made us puppets, two for Ruby and two for me, so we each had one for each hand. They were beasts called trolls, Lydia said; they lived under the mountains or under the sea, she couldn't remember which.

Uncle Hank gave Ruby and me a baseball glove each, and a box of paints, and he gave Lydia a blue dress that was so shimmery she didn't stop kissing him until Ruby made her. Lydia had a small painting for Marcella, and so did I, and so did Ruby—and Uncle Hank gave her an antique jazz record he had found in some store in the Village. The record starred a trombone player, he said, who had once been the best in the world.

When there were no more packages under the tree, Uncle Hank brought out a gold-wrapped box the size of a long shoe. "This is for the house in general, but I'd like Ruby to try guessing what's inside. I'll give you a clue. This thing is half of a pair. I'll keep half with me while I work, and you characters can share the other half here."

"Two boxes of chocolates," Ruby decided.

"No, it's nothing to eat. Here's another clue. It both talks and it listens."

She thought and thought. "A doll?"

"No. And not a bird like Ophelia."

"Give me one more clue."

"All right. The reason I asked *you* to guess, Ruby, is because you're the one who gave me the idea. Hold onto the box, now."

He walked to the front door and closed it behind him. Outside we heard his taxi door slam shut, and then, from the gold-wrapped package, his voice continued as if he were still in the room. "Ruby, you said that with this thing I could talk to Lydia, in the middle of the night when I drove past the house—"

"Like High Boots the policeman! The night we took Santa home!" Ruby tore the gold paper free and pulled out the small plastic box with its stubby antenna, and pushed its button, and shouted "Merry Christmas! Merry Christmas!"

"—And a Happy New Year," said Uncle Hank from the walkie-talkie. "Ho-ho-ho. Can our navigator hear my signal?"

Ruby handed me the walkie-talkie. "Loud and clear," I said. "What's your location, Pilot?"

"Laight Street, Lower Manhattan, far south of the North Pole. This will be my last transmission of the night—I'm going inside now, into the house where my favorite people live. Over."

"Over and out." I went silent, because I was an experienced navigator and knew that the talking stopped when certain things had been said.

But Ruby wasn't so well trained. She grabbed the walkie-talkie and chattered all sorts of nonsense, such as "Wake up, Santa!" and "Talk to me, High Boots!" But she got no reply.

"No more for tonight," said Uncle Hank, in the doorway, his voice coming from his own mouth.

"I want to play radio," Ruby pouted.

"Fine, but no one will call back, because the other radio stays in the taxi, always."

Ruby persisted in holding the button down, calling, "Santa? Are you there, Santa?" But she finally gave up. "Does that *have* to be the rule?"

"Has to be. The other radio stays in the taxi, otherwise the batteries will wear out. And there's one more rule. You two have to share this radio with Lydia. If you don't, how can I tell her—you know—"

"That you *love* her?" smirked Ruby. "How do you know she wants to *hear* that?"

Lydia hugged her red daughter. "Whether I want to hear it is for me to decide. So maybe I won't listen, but maybe I will, to whatever taxi-words fly through the air."

Marcella yawned, which seemed odd, because she was a late-night witch and never yawned before we did. Then she yawned again, so loudly it couldn't be missed. "Gracious me—it's a shame all the presents have been opened."

"Oh," sighed Ruby, "this would be enough presents, if I could play with one radio and Kyle could play with the other."

"But the other radio is in the taxi," Marcella purred. "And the taxi is locked, and it's nearly time for supper. What a shame all the presents have been opened."

"You *said* that." Ruby glared at Marcella. "What's your trick, old witch?"

"Oh, I was wondering if there might be one or two more items hidden somewhere. Didn't you children hear all the banging and clanging on the roof last night?"

"Don't tease." Ruby's frown darkened. "Do you mean to say Santa was here and you didn't wake us up?"

"There wasn't *time,* child. He came and went in a jiffy, and I was asleep myself! Then I heard this clanking and jangling on the roof, this snorting kind of shuffle like cows make, or maybe sheep, or—"

"Reindeer. I don't believe this."

"Well don't, then, but their tracks are all over the roof. I can't imagine what *else* could have made them."

"I'll go look." Ruby jumped to her feet.

"Play detective later. For now, let me finish. Since it was Christmas Eve, and you two are such pals with Santa, I didn't call the cops, but crept up the stairs in my nightie to investigate. And there he stood, beating his knuckles on the roof door, huffing and blowing, his cheeks red as—well, red as cherries. He apologized for not using the chimney. But my stars, how *could* he? We don't *have* a chimney."

Ruby's small amount of patience was gone. "Marcella. Did he leave anything for us?"

"Dear me, I almost forgot! As a matter of fact, he did leave two parcels. Square, fairly stout—"

"And," said Ruby, planted in the center of the room, "do you remember where they are?"

"Well, I really don't seem to recall."

"Marcella."

"Why *now* I have it. I believe I pushed them back in the closet there, back behind my capes—"

Ruby burrowed into the closet and hauled out two large packages, one wrapped in red paper and the other in green.

"He said the red one's for you, but of course you know that already. And he made another comment—a rather curious comment I couldn't figure out—before cramming himself back into that sleigh of his.

Something about how you won't have to sit on so many people now. You'll be more comfortable and so will they."

Ruby shredded ribbons and paper from her parcel, revealing a satin cushion the thickness of three fat telephone books, with the words *Bronx, Brooklyn,* and *Queens* embroidered in gold across its red silky surface. My cushion, when I had it unwrapped, was dark green, and of course was labeled *Staten Island* and *Manhattan.*

"But why," Ruby asked, "is yours so much shorter than mine? You're taller than I am—"

"And that's why. So when we sit on Uncle Hank's front seat, we'll both be as high as he is, but without using phone books. And we won't be sitting on millions of people now, like the night we drove to the North Pole." I noticed something scribbled in tiny black script at the bottom of my cushion. "What's this say, Uncle?"

"Looks like someone's name. Funny writing, isn't it? Couldn't have been an American, to write that way. Looks like it says Foogel, or Foodel, or—"

"Flugel?" I asked.

"Yeah, that must be it. Isn't he one of Santa's pals?"

"From Barbaria," nodded Ruby.

"That's right. And the other one was from Switzerland, where the dogs lug around brandy, and his name was—what was it, Ruby?"

"Fripp." She nodded again, proud of her memory. "And here's his name, down in the corner of *my* thing. No one has to help *me* read it."

"Right," I said, and Uncle Hank grinned to see me make such a good silent joke when I might have said something mean. Then we gathered up our things, gave Ophelia some special Christmas seeds, and went upstairs to our supper.

11

Across the Night

After New Year's Day, the wind roared in from the river, and paper scraps spun across the pavement, and people riding in the cab weren't half so cheerful as before Christmas and didn't tip half so well.

My dad had quit his job and gone away to Texas, to a city called Dallas. He'd found a job with a law firm there, and he left suddenly, as always—and I tried believing it was a regular business trip, but I knew it wasn't.

Mom moved back into the house on Clinton Street, but only to clean it up and make sure it was sold for a good price.

"Don't you think it's time," she asked one afternoon, "for you to move back to Brooklyn?"

"But, Mom," I said carefully, "you're about to move *out* of that house."

"True." She seemed to be speaking as carefully as I was. Luckily for me, I had talked about this moving-back-to-Brooklyn business with Uncle Hank, and had some ideas ready so I wouldn't hurt Mom's feelings.

"How soon," I asked, "will you move out?"

"As soon as I have a buyer and find a new apartment, someplace classy enough for a lady banker and a big boy."

We were walking near Marcella's house, on the promenade along the Hudson River, and I was glad to be able to look down into the water. Ever since Marcella had taught me to search in the river, it had helped me see all sorts of things.

"Don't you think," I said, watching a piece of wood float toward the shore, "that I should stay in school here, at least until third grade ends?"

"You like your new school." Mom ran a hand through my hair. "And you like Ruby and Lydia."

"Yeah. And Marcella. She's old but she's still my friend. And she isn't feeling well. She's weaker all the time—and she says Ruby's a comfort to her, and me too."

"I'm sure you are. But I hope you realize, Kyle, that you're a comfort to *me,* as well."

"I *am?*"

"Of course you are."

"I'm not just a—bother?" I'd done it again; Mom was crying. She cried a lot in those cold weeks after Christmas. "Not just a bother for a lady banker?"

"No, Darling. Don't ever say that. But if you're truly happy in your new school, I suppose you should stay until its year ends."

Now I was crying, too. Maybe cold wind and a cold river make everyone cry. I was crying, but was glad I wouldn't have to leave Ruby's house until summer vacation began. I held Mom's hand. "But we can be together—we can be together lots."

"That's right, Sweetie. Every day when I finish work. But I'm so *cold,* all of a sudden. Shall we walk back and have some cocoa?"

"That sounds lovely," I said, and she laughed, as I knew she would, since *that sounds lovely* was one of her favorite things to say. We turned and started toward the house on Laight Street.

So I saw Mom nearly every day, for a few minutes at least. But Dad was far off in Texas, and I never saw him at all. He sent me a few expensive presents and some funny cards I stuck on my wall in the room next to Ruby's—but he didn't come back to New York. Where he went instead, on his first vacation, was to Colorado. Uncle Hank showed me where it was located on our map, and he didn't say so, but I could see for myself that Colorado was even farther away than Texas.

One afternoon when Ruby and I got back from school, a postcard waited for me on the table beside Marcella's armchair. Hank and Lydia were there, too—they all sat watching me read it.

First I looked at the picture, which showed a tiny house on the side of a snowy mountain. Then I read Dad's writing. "What," I asked Marcella, "is a chalet?"

"It's that house," she said, breathing hard. "In the photo. With the steep roof." For a long minute she listened to her Christmas record as it played from the corner. The trombone sounded like it was singing about something that had been lost. "A chalet is a ski house." She took a deep breath. "—Where people stay. When they're on a vacation in the mountains."

I read the card again. "Dad says he's *buying* this ski house. But don't ski houses cost money?"

"Lots," whispered Marcella. Across the room, Uncle Hank looked up from reading his book. He smiled at her, but his smile didn't look happy.

"Mom says he doesn't *have* any money. At least, not much. Not enough to buy a house—"

"But there are many ways—" Marcella breathed out very slowly. "—Many ways to buy a house."

Uncle Hank propped the book in his lap and watched her.

"It's hard to understand," she whispered, "why some people choose what they choose."

We waited for her to say more, but she didn't say anything; she fell asleep there in her armchair, with the trombone playing its blue and purple notes. At least I thought she was asleep, until Lydia crossed the room and checked on her and motioned to Uncle Hank. He knelt and listened to Marcella's heart.

"No." He looked at me, then at Ruby, who was studying my postcard. "Marcella isn't asleep. She's dead."

Just like that. She didn't seem to be dead, like on TV where they have their eyes open and their necks crooked. She had her eyes closed and seemed to be listening to the music. When the record ended, Lydia turned it over and let the other side play, since it was Marcella's favorite record and we always let the other side play. Then Lydia and Uncle Hank lifted Marcella onto the bed, and Ruby lit some candles, and we listened to some sad music and some happy music, and we watched Marcella's face.

"She's the most wonderful witch there is," said Ruby from Lydia's lap.

"The most wonderful there *was,*" I corrected. "She's dead now. She's gone."

"But she's right here, stupid." Ruby pointed. "I could touch her, if I wanted to."

"And do you want to?" I held Uncle Hank's hand.

"No. She's cold, Lydia says. I won't touch her if she's cold."

"Me neither. She's cold because she's dead. Gone."

"Is *not.* She won't be gone until they burn her and throw her ashes in the river. Right, Lydia?"

"Darling, you're both right. She's dead, and she's cold, and she's gone and yet she isn't gone. She'll never be gone unless we forget her."

"And," said Uncle Hank, "we won't forget her. Who could forget such a wise witch?" He bent over Marcella and kissed her cold forehead.

Then he went to the kitchen, and I heard him phoning a place he called the coroner's office. Soon a doctor arrived to sign a paper saying Marcella was dead, and his men carried her out on a covered stretcher to the ambulance. Uncle Hank climbed in and sat beside the stretcher; the door closed and they drove away to the place where Marcella's body would be put into the furnace and turned to ashes.

And that was when it finally seemed real—when the ambulance drove east to Hudson Street and disappeared. Then we saw that Marcella was truly gone, and we cried, holding onto each other like babies lost in the subway.

But even that sort of crying had to end sometime, and when it did, Lydia made us cinnamon toast and hot chocolate and said that going for a walk would help us feel better. Ruby asked if we could walk by the river.

"It's terribly cold over there, Darling. On Franklin

Street the buildings will shield us from the wind. But by the river—"

"The river is Marcella's place to go when she needs answers. *Please?*"

"All right, we'll walk to the river. But dress warmly."

"I can still wear red, can't I?"

"Wear what you wish, but be sure it's warm."

So Ruby wore her red parka, and we walked stiffly to the river—and for the first time I noticed that Lydia did limp, just as Ruby had claimed. It was from the cold, I told myself, that she limped. But I knew it was also from the pain—I mean, the pain in her heart—because I felt like limping myself. We gazed at the gray flowing Hudson and held onto each other, and then we trudged home, with the wind at our backs and the sun almost down.

Soon Marcella was only ashes in a stone jar on Lydia's shelf. We would scatter the ashes on the river, Lydia promised. Not yet, but soon. When the moon was full.

I slept on my cot in Ruby's room, because although we fought sometimes and argued often, neither of us wanted to sleep alone. Lydia said I could have Marcella's bed now, but I remembered Marcella lying there and preferred sharing a room with Ruby.

But Uncle Hank wasn't scared of Marcella's bed; sometimes we found him snoring in it when we went off to school. He might wake up long enough to say hello and pinch our noses, but then he rolled over and went back to sleep. He had been up half the night driving around New York, and was still tired.

We would leave him there and Lydia would walk us to school. I went to Ruby's school now, not my old school in Brooklyn. We walked down Hudson Street, through the blowing bits of grime, and when we talked, we talked about Marcella, because she was in everything we saw.

January was a raw freezing month, of mittens and boots and runny noses. And a lonely month, but not so lonely as it might have been, for every night—after bedtime, and after Lydia's stories of Biff and Baff the dolphins who carried underwater balloons—every night Lydia brought out the walkie-talkie and set it on the table between our beds. And then, when she turned down the light and left us, we waited for Uncle Hank's voice.

Sometimes he had telephoned earlier to say he was at one of the airports or way up in Westchester, too many miles for his radio voice to cross. Even police walkie-talkies could only signal for a mile or two; Uncle Hank had to be close for his radio to reach us. But when he was close, and knew we lay waiting in the dark, he always pushed down his button and talked across the night.

"You there, Navigator?"

"Roger, Pilot." I knelt beside Ruby's bed, so she could hear him too. "Home Base receives you loud and clear. What's your location?"

"Church and Chambers, headed north to the bright lights."

Ruby pressed the button. "Any passengers, Pilot?"

"Hey there, Little Red. Yeah, a couple of astronauts. But they're dressed in business suits and claim to be advertising men, so they might be spies."

"Well, make sure they give you a big tip."

This brought laughter from Uncle Hank and from voices we didn't know. Then he said, "We're crossing Spring Street—your signal's getting weak, I'll have to sign off. Good night, Scarlet. Good night, Navigator."

"Night, Pilot. Be careful—"

"I will, don't worry. Over."

"Over and out," called Ruby, who had earned the rank of Radio Operator First Class.

She laid the walkie-talkie on the table, and I crept back to bed, and we drifted into that place between being awake and being asleep where we discussed astronauts who were spies and dolphins who carried balloons . . . until the fish wore helmets and the rockets swam in the sea and we slipped into our dreams to sort everything out.

In the morning the walkie-talkie was never where we had put it, but upstairs where Lydia lay sleeping. Usually it sat on the table beside her bed, but sometimes it was snuggled right in bed with her, its switch still turned on, as if it were her magic bear and she waited for it to speak.

We would wake her, and tease her for wanting to hear Uncle Hank's voice, and then we'd have breakfast and walk to school.

The moon whittled itself down to a sliver, and almost disappeared, and then started growing fat. Often we spoke to Ruby of Marcella's wish that when the moon was full we should scatter her ashes on the river. Lydia explained what Marcella had said about life beginning as a mountain stream and ending in the peaceful ocean, and she explained how cramped a graveyard would feel compared to the wide ease of the sea.

"But," Ruby argued, "do we have to throw her in the *ocean?*"

"Not necessarily," Lydia answered, her voice low and calm. "We can also scatter her ashes in the river she loved, here right near our house, and let the river carry them out into the ocean for us. I think that might be simplest and best—"

Ruby shivered as if a cold wind had blown through the room. Then she stamped off to whisper with Ophelia.

Every night as the moon grew more round, Ruby grew more and more quiet, until one night she didn't even talk on the radio to Uncle Hank. And then, on the day the moon would turn full, she revealed her own plan for Marcella's ashes.

It was a Saturday, so blowy and cold that the wind made people stagger in miserable zigzags along the sidewalk. After lunch Ruby and I stayed inside. She took me to her room, and we played with our Christmas puppets.

"I'm tired of this," she said all at once. "This full moon is terrible—only Ophelia understands me. Not you, not those grown-ups. I'm going downstairs to talk with my bird."

"Okay." I watched her stamp away and pretended my feelings weren't hurt. My boy puppet hit my girl puppet on the head, but that didn't help, so I took them up to Lydia's studio where she was painting a picture of a blue-bearded man. She didn't mind my being there unless I talked too much, and this time I didn't talk at all, except a few secrets I whispered to the boy puppet. Lydia painted, and from time to time smiled across at me, but said nothing. Not until Uncle Hank arrived did we guess anything might be wrong.

"Where's Ruby?" he asked. "In her room?"

"No, Uncle, she got in one of her moods—went downstairs to talk with the parrot."

"She wasn't there when I came in. Are you sure?"

"Yes, Uncle." It had been such a cold shut-in month

that everyone was touchy. "She said no one understands her but Ophelia."

"It's strange I didn't see her."

"Maybe," I sighed, "she's up on the roof being a winter ballerina again. I'll go look."

"Thanks, Kid. And I'll look in the basement."

Now I knew he was worried. The basement was famous for its rats and baby alligators; no one went down there without a serious reason. But he didn't find Ruby in the basement and I didn't find her on the roof, and Lydia didn't find her anywhere else. Then Uncle Hank noticed that her red parka and boots were gone.

"Has she ever run away before? I mean, outside the house?"

"Never." Lydia held her face in both hands. "But she's never seen anyone die before, either. These last weeks, she's been so quiet—exactly what did she say, Kyle?"

"That no one understands her but Ophelia. And something about the full moon being terrible."

"But she *loves* the full moon! Marcella said that every month its ghost would visit—"

"Sure," said Uncle Hank. "But tonight's a different sort of full moon, if we're putting those ashes in the river."

"How *stupid* of me! I got to painting and forgot all about the ashes. But the jar's still on the shelf—"

"The jar's here." Uncle Hank shook it. "But the ashes are gone, so she must have decided to protect them from us. Put on your coats—we've got to find her before dark."

In the taxi we crisscrossed every alley in the neighborhood, asking strangers if they had seen a red little girl. We drove past our school, and past her favorite playground, and were on our way to the ice cream store when I remembered.

"Lydia, was the walkie-talkie in your room when we left the house?"

"I'm not sure. No, I don't think so."

"Then she took it with her."

"But why would she, if she's running away?"

"Because she's a show-off." I felt bad calling Ruby that, even if we all knew it was true. But it made me angry to see Lydia and Uncle Hank so worried, and to feel so worried myself. "*Any* kid would want to show off, running away on a cold day like this." I opened the glove compartment and took out Uncle Hank's walkie-talkie.

"Wait a minute, Kyle. Put in a new battery—it's in a plastic bag, way back there."

So I changed the battery, and leaned out the window into the freezing wind, and pushed the button. "You hear me, Ruby?"

First there was only static, even with the volume

turned high. Then a few words came across, a few weak words only I understood.

"She said *octopus,* Uncle! And eel! I know where she is—go back the other way!"

Scowling, he made a fast U-turn against the traffic and drove us across Franklin Street to Hudson, then north a block, where he signaled to turn left.

"No, Uncle! Straight up to Canal!" I leaned out the window into the biting cold wind and pushed the button. "Ruby, do you read me?"

"Won't tell." Her voice was louder now, which meant we were close—but it was also slower and thicker and sounded almost drunk. "Won't tell where. Won't leave Marcella alone. Won't let . . . won't let you take her . . . away. So cold."

"Left on Canal!" I shouted to Uncle Hank, and I didn't have to tell him how frozen Ruby must be, or that he had to go through the red lights. When she spoke again, her words were slower than before. "Kyle. Remember . . . Halloween?"

"I remember. You teased me and told me to be an octopus. Or an eel. But I don't *want* to be an octopus, Ruby, and neither do you. *Do* you?"

"No." She seemed to be working hard to make any sound. "Nuh-No. D-Don't want to. No."

"Ruby? *Ruby?*"

"Not so cold." Her voice seemed closer now, but almost asleep. "Not so . . . cold. Not . . . so . . ." And she went silent. I called again and again but nothing came back.

Uncle Hank blasted us through the screeching traffic of the West Side Highway, and veered left where I pointed, and stopped beside the long dock where Marcella had brought Ruby and me just before Halloween.

But there was no one on the dock. No cold spot of red, only a copper sun sinking behind New Jersey.

"She's there, Uncle. She has to be." And I ran out onto the rotten planks of the pier, dodging the holes that would drop me into the river, hoping as hard as I could hope that Ruby hadn't dropped into the river herself. I ran onto the pier because there was no time to explain it to the others. The taxi doors slammed and they ran after me.

I knew exactly where to go—to the edge of the dock where Marcella had taken us the day Ruby and I peeked down and saw our reflections in the river and decided to be desert explorers for Halloween. I knew where to go, but I couldn't understand why Ruby wasn't there on the dock waiting for me.

Then I reached the edge and looked over, and saw, yes, she *had* waited, but not in our same spot. A wooden ladder disappeared into the river, which on this winter day was not flat and peaceful but wild with brown foam. On the side of the ladder, three or four feet above the spraying waves, someone had nailed a platform hardly bigger than a bookshelf. And on this shelf, feet dangling above the waves, sat a red bundle clutching a paper bag in one arm and a walkie-talkie in the other.

"Ruby!" I shouted down, lowering myself onto the first rung down. The ladder looked like it had been made of wood left over from the Revolutionary War. "Ruby?"

She was asleep, or seemed to be, and heard nothing. Asleep the same way Marcella had been asleep—

I looked back across the dark, oily-smelling pier, which seemed to sway from the force of the waves, and saw Uncle Hank racing across its plank surface toward me. Far behind him ran Lydia, shouting something I couldn't hear through the wind. I had time to go down just one more rung before Uncle Hank caught my arms and pulled me back onto the dock and told me to stay right there and be careful. Then he made his way down the ladder, testing each rotten-looking rung before putting his weight on it.

When he reached Ruby, he stuffed the walkie-talkie in one pocket and the bag of ashes in the other. The wind howled across the river, then twisted to a higher note when it whistled under the pier. Uncle buttoned the top of Ruby's coat, then took off his belt and used it to lash her into the belly of his coat. Even more cautiously than before, he hoisted himself—with Ruby in his bulging pouch—up the ladder away from the dirty waves.

"She's breathing," he said. "Barely. Let's get her to the car." And then he was gone, running in great long strides with Ruby hugged inside his coat.

Lydia limped so badly when she ran that she slowed me down. When we reached the taxi, Uncle Hank had Ruby on the back seat, and was blowing into her mouth, then pressing her chest to make her breathe out, then blowing in again. It was terrible to see her there beyond the plexiglass partition, not moving at all, lying on the sagging seat where passengers were meant to sit. Her eyes were shut and her skin was blue.

Lydia took her from Uncle Hank; he jumped in the front seat beside me, and honked the horn and headed straight up the West Side Highway, on the wrong side of the road, until we could cross over at Canal Street and go really fast. No red light stopped us that trip—we must have made it to St. Vincent's Hospital in four minutes, but I was too scared by the blueness of Ruby's face to check Hoboken Time. In the back seat Lydia breathed into Ruby's mouth and pushed her chest, and breathed in again, over and over and over. At last, when I was starting to think nothing in her blue face could ever change, Ruby coughed and gasped and coughed again. But still her eyes wouldn't open.

We stayed in the hospital all that night, and never did see the woman in the moon. But at one o'clock, when they let us into Ruby's room, she had her eyes open, and her skin glowed beautifully dark again, not blue and waxy like before.

It was dawn when Uncle Hank drove me back to Laight Street, and told me I was the New York City hero of the night, and told me he loved me, which he had never said in quite that same voice. Maybe it was from all the excitement of Ruby's running away, or from waiting in the shiny white hall of the hospital, but when he said he loved me, I cried and cried and wasn't the least bit embarrassed.

When I woke up, the sun was shining, and Uncle Hank had bacon sizzling on the stove, and the stone jar sat on its shelf, full of ashes again—but the best thing of all sat in Lydia's kitchen cupboard: a golden fresh crumb cake, delivered in the night, as always, by the woman in the moon.

Epilogue

There are millions and millions of people in New York City. So the chance of meeting just the perfect person, at just the perfect moment, doesn't seem great. But it can happen. I know, because it happened to me. In Uncle Hank's taxi, on the rainiest Sunday of the spring, at the corner of Fulton and Pearl.

We were fishing for tourists and trying to be cheerful—but there were no tourists in our cab and not much cheer, either. There was rain outside, where the tourists were hiding, and gloom inside, where we tried not to think of Ruby's great sadness.

On the awful night back in January, she hadn't quite frozen to death—but she had never quite thawed out either. For months, through the coldest of the winter, Ruby refused to speak of Marcella or of Marcella's ashes or of the full moon or of very much else. Every morning she still walked to school with Lydia and me, and she still wore her red dresses and blouses and pants and shoes—but she wouldn't joke and scold in her old naughty way. We were so worried about her, Uncle Hank and I, that when we went riding together on Sunday afternoons we tried to discuss anything else. Even my parents' divorce—supposed to take place in just a few months—was easier to think about than Ruby being so quiet.

So now, this Sunday in May, we watched the windshield wipers slosh the rain back and forth, and we talked about all the songs we should invent, and all the tourist-fish we couldn't catch.

"This is the spot," said Uncle Hank. "Right here—exactly the best spot for snagging fat tourists."

"I don't see any." The Pearl Street sidewalk was very wet and very empty.

"Oh, they're out there, swimming from one restaurant to another—and they'll be fun to catch, you wait and see."

"Okay, Uncle." But all I saw was the side window with its dribbles of water that reminded me of Ruby's unhappiness. "Why will it be fun to snag these tourists?"

"Because once we catch them, we can zip onto the FDR Drive and zoom uptown at fifty thousand miles an hour, and deliver them to their ritzy hotels, and make twelve bucks in ten minutes."

We glided between a lobster place on our left and a crab place on our right. "But Uncle, where *are* these tourist-fish?"

"Good question." He peered through the flap-flap of our wipers. "Fish are supposed to love the rain. Wait, there's one. But is he a tourist, Navigator?"

"Don't know. He sure is fat, though."

"Well then, we'll scoop him up."

The man, under his shiny black umbrella, didn't have a hand in the air, but we pulled up to him—slowly, to keep from splashing his legs.

"A byoo-tee-full day!" he shouted as he flopped inside. "A luffly day in port!" I knew he wasn't from New York, since he liked the rain—and he wasn't American, since he talked funny. "Take me pliss," he bellowed, "take me to Brooklyn!"

I looked at Uncle Hank and he looked at me, and we laughed good-bye to our quick twelve dollars.

"Are you a tourist?" I asked the man.

"Very fonny, my boy." Joining our laughter, he boomed hard enough to shake the cab. "A *toorist! Good* one!" He slapped his heavy sides.

"Tourists," I explained, "don't live in Brooklyn. That's why I was asking—"

"Live in Brooklyn? Very *fonny!* Very *good* one!" He laughed until tears splattered his cheeks. "I live no place, my boy. At least no place on land. I go to Brooklyn because my boat lies in Brooklyn making repairs.

My *ship*. I am captain, my boy, of a Greek ship. So I go to Brooklyn. You like to see my ship? Is only a freighter, but—"

"Maybe—" First I looked over to check with Uncle Hank. "I mean, we should be making money, shouldn't we, Uncle? —From all the wet tourists?"

"Oh, a Greek ship sounds pretty sharp to me—makes me think of all the cruises I haven't made, all the islands I haven't seen. Anyway, where *are* all those tourists?"

"Swimming in some other stream."

"So!" said our passenger. "You shall visit my ship?"

"Yes," I said. "Yes, *please,* Captain."

And so began our friendship with Captain Fyorek, the perfect person at the perfect time. While we drove across the bridge with our wipers slapping, the captain rumbled that *he* didn't mind the wet, he *loved* the wet, the wet was his life because he lived in the saltiest, wettest wet of all, the ocean.

And as he laughed into the rain, I saw Ruby's face in my mind—and saw it not sad, the way it had been all winter, but as sparkling as it had looked during the fall, whenever some new idea was about to pop from her head. And the reason I saw her with that look was that I was starting to hatch a pretty good idea of my own. Captain Fyorek laughed some more, and the idea grew inside me—but I didn't say anything yet, because

I knew it was such a large idea that it needed time, like a large crumb cake in an oven needs time, before it could be brought out and tasted.

We drove through my old neighborhood, down Henry Street to Atlantic Avenue, then west to the docks, and the captain laughed the whole wet way—and the whole way I thought of Ruby's face, with all its different moods, and turned my idea carefully in my mind, and it looked better from each new side. We parked the taxi on the dock, which in Brooklyn was made of cement, polished and clean, not rotten wood like the dock in Manhattan where Ruby had nearly frozen. Captain Fyorek showed us the ramp leading into his ship and held his umbrella over us as we made our way across.

"Called gangplank." He stamped his feet on the metal ramp, making it echo. "And this floor of ship is called main deck. And my cabin, where we shall have our delicious hot drink out of the wet, is this way pliss, Kyle and Mister Hank."

For he had learned our names, and had learned I was a navigator and Uncle Hank was my pilot. He said his ship had a navigator too, with lots of charts, just as I had Uncle Hank's map book showing all the streets and boroughs of New York.

We looked out the round window of his room, and we drank glasses of hot spiced wine—mine was mostly hot water—and we spoke of many things while I turned my new idea around and around with growing satisfaction.

"Captain Fyorek, how many days is it before—well, before your ship—"

"Before we sail? Eleven days, my boy! So I have still eleven days in your wet city. You take me to footbol game, yes?"

"No," I laughed, and was glad to see Uncle Hank laugh, too. "Football doesn't start for a long time. Now there's just baseball." I wanted to ask, but couldn't.

"Bezball! But bezball is good! The bezball game where you take me will be *wonnerful,* yes?"

I looked across at Uncle Hank, who grinned at me and nodded. "Yes, Captain—I'm sure baseball would be fun for all of us." Through the cabin window, the lights of Manhattan were dim and far away. "But, Captain—"

"Yes, my boy Kyle?"

"When you sail, where will you go?"

"To country of Portugal!" He seemed happy at the thought of the place, although its name didn't make me happy since it wasn't what I wanted to hear. "Port of Lisbon. Byoo-tee-full! Such wine, such prettiest women!" He smiled at Uncle Hank, who smiled happily back.

"And then where?" It might be unlucky to ask the name I wanted to hear, so I asked a different one. "Then you'll go to—Switzerland?"

"No, my boy." The captain laughed till he hugged his broad chest. "No salty wet in Switzerland. No sea, only mountains and yodeling. Next after Lisbon, we put in at Tangier. Also byoo-tee-full. In country of Morocco." He laughed some more, but stopped when he saw my face. "But why do you look at me like this, Kyle? Why so surprised?"

"Because I'm glad." The idea was so nearly ready, I had to share it with him and Uncle Hank. But there was one more question. "Captain Fyorek, you say your ship carries freight. Does it ever carry—passengers? Like a taxi carries passengers?"

"Sometimes yes." His eyes were serious now. "Sometimes, but not so many times. Only with special—circumstance? The boss in Greece must give approval. The owner. But he is good man, and I work for him many long years. He is Fyorek's friend." The captain glanced at Uncle Hank, then back to me. "So—what is your, ah, circumstance, Navigator Kyle?"

Finally I told him. About Marcella the purple witch, who had died and was now ashes, and about Ruby the tiny red witch who had almost died because of the ashes.

"Ruby knows Marcella wanted to end in the ocean, but she doesn't like the ocean enough to let it *have* Marcella. I mean, she *tries* to like the ocean, but she's scared of it, and—oh, I can't explain this right."

"You explain very good. But it is a big matter." Captain Fyorek looked at my uncle again; Uncle Hank nodded firmly. "A *very* big matter. So I must meet your witch Ruby. You say she wants to sail to Morocco?"

"I *know* she does. And so does Lydia, since she was born there. And Uncle Hank wants to go *anywhere,* so long as it's far away and fun."

"Nephew," said my uncle, "you are brilliant. In fact you're the smartest navigator I've ever known."

"Really? But—do you think we can do it?"

"Maybe so. Maybe not. There's your mother to consider, with all her high hopes for your education—"

"That's right. She'll never let me go."

"Now, wait a minute—I didn't say she won't let you go. But it may not be easy to persuade her."

"She won't let me. But don't *you* want to go?"

"I think maybe I do." Uncle Hank smiled. "Let's wait and see what happens."

And Uncle was right, the arrangements were pretty tricky.

First my mom was completely against the trip. Completely. She talked about how seasick I would be, throwing up all the way across the ocean. Then she talked about all the strange diseases I would catch in Morocco. But mostly she talked about the months of school I would miss.

Still, Uncle Hank never gave up. Three days after meeting Captain Fyorek, we were cruising Seventh Avenue. He rolled down his window, took a breath of spring air, and said, "The more I think about it, the more restless I feel."

"Restless?"

"Itchy. Impatient to be moving. And the more restless I feel in New York, the more I want to sail to Morocco."

"With a beautiful dark woman?"

"That sounds good. And with some beautiful kids."

"But how about Mom? How does *she* feel when you get—restless? And when I do?"

"Don't worry about your mom." Uncle Hank smiled across Seventh Avenue toward the windows of a store called Barneys. "She sounds tough now, sure. But I'll keep working on her. She likes museums?"

"Mom *loves* museums—you know that."

"Fine. The country of Morocco, when I'm done painting it for her, will look like a huge museum—a museum so gorgeous her son shouldn't miss his chance to see it."

"Maybe."

"Just wait," said Uncle Hank. "I'll work on her."

And later that evening, when Mom stopped at Ruby's house for a visit, I listened while Uncle Hank tried painting his museum idea for her. He sounded very grown-up, using words I didn't know too well. First he told her about the *architecture* of Morocco, with its

Moorish *elements* and wonderful array of colors . . . and then he talked about North African music, which used some wild-sounding instruments I couldn't pronounce . . .

"Germs," said my mom. She had her arms crossed over her stomach as if she wanted to block out any picture of beautiful buildings or music or colors. She looked around to be sure Lydia was out of the room, since she liked Lydia and would never have said bad things about Lydia's birthplace. "Too many germs. In Morocco, from what I've heard, germs are everywhere."

"I didn't get sick once," said Uncle Hank, "and I lived with those germs for over a year."

"You're not a child," she said, and I knew we could never win her vote.

"And then," beamed Uncle Hank, as if he hadn't noticed the interruption, "—there's Moroccan cuisine."

"Moroccan *what?*" asked Ruby from her perch in the corner next to Ophelia's cage.

Uncle and Mom both turned to look at Ruby, they were so surprised to hear her speak.

"Moroccan cuisine," whispered my mom, who loved food from all over the world. "Wonderful Moroccan food."

"Doesn't *it* have *germs,* too?" Ruby was actually trying to smile! Teasing my mom with one of her jokes!

"Germs," Mom repeated thoughtfully. "I suppose germs are everywhere, even in Manhattan."

"But finally," whispered Uncle Hank, "there's the lovely Arabic language, which is spoken all across North Africa—but nowhere as beautifully as in Morocco."

"Is it as beautiful," asked Ruby, "as Lydia?"

The room was so quiet that at first we heard only the scratch of Ophelia pecking at her feathers. Then, from Lydia's studio upstairs, we heard the faraway strains of strange music. For the first time, I wondered if it was Moroccan.

"Yes, Ruby—that's exactly how beautiful Arabic is. As beautiful as Lydia. But in over a year, being such an old guy, I had trouble learning to speak Arabic. My ears aren't as quick for a new language as some younger ears might be."

"Whose ears?" Ruby looked around the room, first at me, then at Uncle Hank, and finally at my mom.

"*Your* ears," said Mom. "Yours and my boy Kyle's." She studied the framed photo, on the piano, of Marcella zooming along on her roller skates, white hair streaming behind her. "I suppose Marcella would have wanted you both to learn Arabic. It's just that the ocean seems so—big."

"Yeah," said Uncle Hank. "It can be a scary idea, the ocean."

"Scary," Ruby asked, "for somebody's ashes?"

"Scary in lots of ways. But Captain Fyorek can teach us about the tides, and the waves, and everything else, and then we won't be so scared."

"I guess so," said Ruby. She gazed up at Ophelia to see what she might say—but Ophelia, for once, was silent.

"I guess so too," said my mom. "I guess all of us could be less scared."

"*So* then," I said quickly, as my dad liked to do. "It's settled."

"Yes," nodded Mom. "I suppose it is."

And that was when I knew my cake was out of the oven and was golden brown and tasted even better than I had hoped possible.

There were still lots of details, as adults like to say, to be straightened out. Captain Fyorek, once he had talked with Mom and Lydia, had to call the owner of his ship for permission. Uncle Hank had to get back the deposit money on his Ninth Street apartment. And Lydia, as the new owner of Marcella's house, had to find someone she could rent it to while we were away. But even that wasn't such a big problem. She rented it to my mom!

"When the weather gets nice and hot," Ruby instructed, "just put all the ferns and green things up on my roof. That's where they're happiest."

"Let's go take a look," said Mom.

Off they went up the stairs—and when they came back down, eighteen minutes later, Mom was telling Ruby about money.

"We're discussing *income,* "Mom told Lydia, who was serving slices of blueberry pie. "Ruby wanted to know how money works, and I was saying that income won't be a problem during your trip. For one thing, you'll have my rent money—"

"And Uncle Hank's taxi money," I said, "that he's out making right now."

"Yes," smiled Lydia. "And I have a few dimes hidden away—and Morocco isn't such an expensive place, for those of us who know what's what."

"So don't worry about money," said Mom. "The money will turn up, if you keep my boy as happy as he is now."

This amazed me. "You mean you don't mind my missing the end of school?"

"School shmool. When you come back you'll speak Arabic, you'll know all about the ocean and the stars—you'll be able to *teach* school."

"That isn't what Dad would say."

"Dad shmad. Dad's in Texas."

"There's the spirit," said Lydia, her eyes wide with wonder.

"If you and Hank and Ruby look after my son," said Mom, "I'll look after Ophelia the talking bird."

We served Ophelia a slice of pie, and served another small slice for each of us, and felt very much pleased with ourselves.

The tugboats backed us into the harbor and tooted good-bye, and Captain Fyorek blasted his whistle back at them, echoing off the Wall Street skyscrapers. We passed Governor's Island and the Statue of Liberty and the Staten Island ferryboat. Then Brooklyn slid by on our left and Staten Island on our right, until finally we cruised under the Verrazano-Narrows Bridge and Captain Fyorek showed me and Ruby how to give the order for full power. She used his private phone to call the order down to the Chief Engineer's room; soon the propeller went faster, and we speeded up and were out on the open sea.

Three days went by, and Ruby wasn't bored and neither was I, since we had so much to learn about engines and charts and long waves called swells, and kitchens called galleys.

Each subject had its own special room and special expert. The thundering engine room, with its diesel pistons going up-and-down, up-and-down in long mechanical rows, was run by a Frenchman named Maurice who wore a tiny mustache and spoke with an accent kind of like Lydia's. His fingers were stained dark from the oil of his machinery, but he seemed very clean in everything he did, and was very patient, explaining each machine to us over and over.

The First Cook, a skinny man named Franz, taught us the best way to peel potatoes, using a special peeler he had bought years and years earlier in Germany and he also taught us to yodel.

But most fun for me was the chart room, where Captain Fyorek explained all the different maps of so many different places. And so many *kinds* of maps! I had never guessed, for example, that the ocean went just as deep *down* as any mountain went *up,* or that the different kinds of waves could be caused by how deep or shallow the sea was beneath them.

He even had maps of the sky. At night—my favorite time on his ship—we had the stars. Captain Fyorek gave us lessons in what he called heavenly navigation, pointing to all the animals covered in jewels who moved across the sky and sparkled a thousand times more brightly than all the lights of Broadway.

And the moon. There had never been such a moon, growing riper each night just beyond our reach. And on the fourth night, when it was full, Ruby knew the time had come to do what we had to do. No one needed to tell her.

We stood at the stern—which on a ship means the back end—and watched the moon gazing down, so sad and happy and tender, so much bigger than any New York moon.

"Navigator Kyle to the bridge," I called, for we hadn't forgotten our walkie-talkies and had given the pilot's radio, on this voyage, to Captain Fyorek.

"I read you, Navigator Kyle. Is it time to slow down the screw?"

"Yes, please, Captain." My watch, so clear in the light of the full moon, said Hoboken Time was exactly twelve past midnight. "All engines slow."

"Roger," he called. "All slow." In the pause that followed, we knew he was talking to Maurice in the engine room. Within seconds the giant propeller vibrated the deck slower and slower until the engine had dropped to a low steady beat, and the ship slowed itself in the ocean, and the wind dropped to a calm sweet breeze.

"Captain calling Witch Ruby."

"Hello, Captain." Ruby beamed toward the bridge, then turned to smile up at the moon as if she were a red princess of the sky.

"Are you—happy, Miss Ruby?"

"Yes, Captain. I've never been so happy, even at Christmas."

"Not too—sad?" asked the Captain's radio voice, while Uncle and Lydia and I watched Ruby and remembered the coldest night of our lives. "Not too sad about ashes of old lady the witch?"

"Not sad." Ruby smiled into the sky. "I'm ready now, and she's ready now, up in the moon, and so are these ashes." Ruby dipped a handful of cindery gray ashes from her paper bag and dropped them over the railing. "They should go into the sea, these ashes. It's what Marcella wanted."

"Good," said Captain Fyorek from the walkie-talkie. We could see his smile in the sound of his voice. "Ashes will follow us, and will go everyplace there is ocean. Everyplace you look, and see ocean, there is your Marcella. And in the moon, too! Lucky witch, Marcella."

"Yes," said Ruby. "Me, too."

She smiled, and we all smiled as we took handfuls of ashes from the paper bag, and watched them scatter into the sea. When the ashes were all gone, drifting to every part of the world, I told the Captain we were ready for full power, just as he had told his Chief Engineer when we left New York. He gave the order and we sailed east through the stars, through the waves, through the smiles of the witch in the sky.